UNWRITTEN RUNES

A PARANORMAL NOVELLA DUOLOGY

KD CASEY

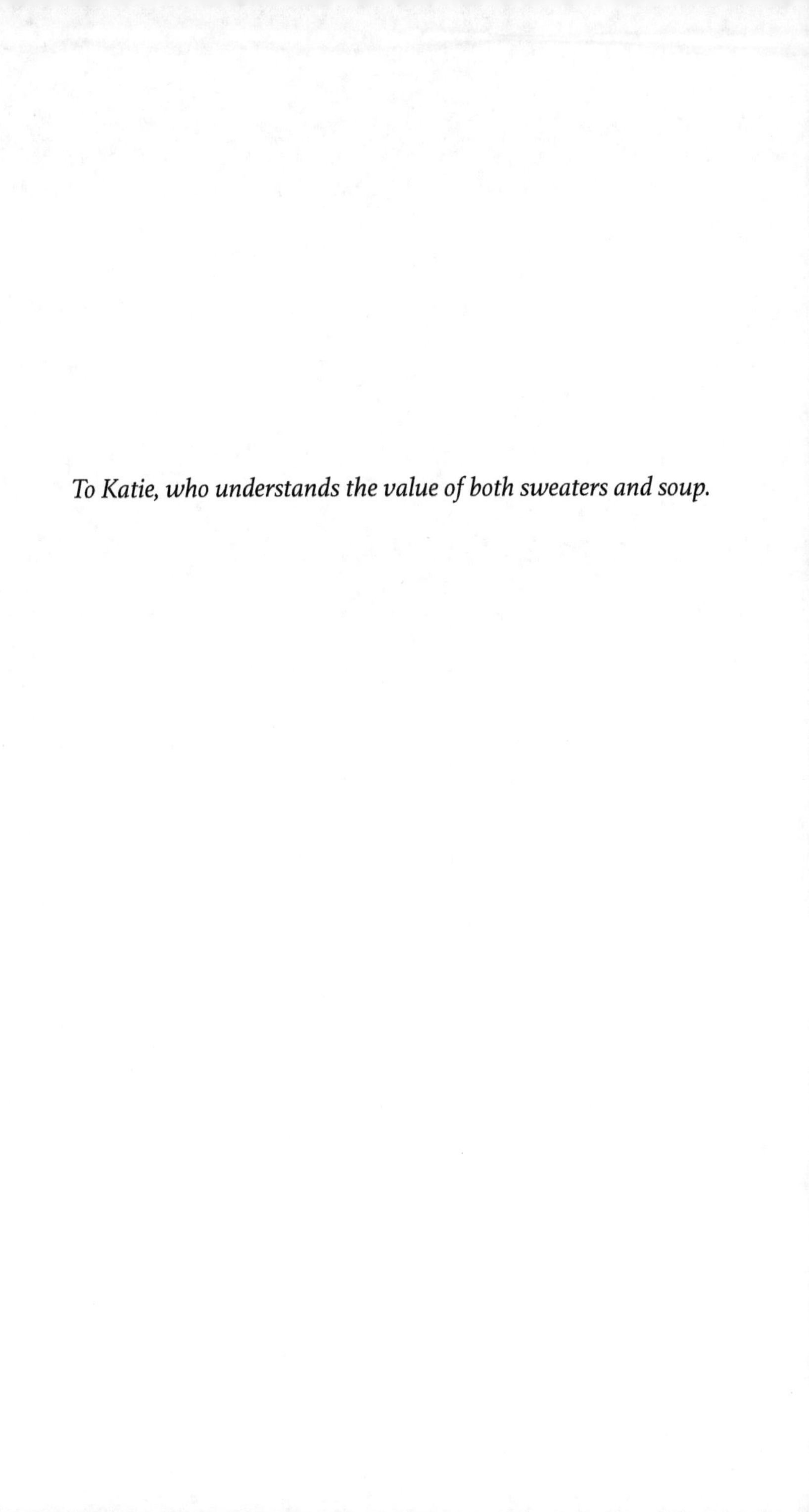

To Katie, who understands the value of both sweaters and soup.

FOREWORD

Several Halloweens ago, a few other writers and I began the Spooky Season Challenge. The task was to re-imagine a scene from a book but incorporate supernatural elements. These were supposed to be short stories...but as is usual with my writing, what started as a fun idea evolved into something much longer. In this case, these two novellas: *Unwritten Runes* and *Ordinary Ghosts*. While these use characters from the *Unwritten Rules* 'verse, they are standalone paranormal M/M romances with some Jewish elements.

Portions of the profits from these novellas will go to SMYAL, an organization near and dear to my heart that creates opportunities for LGBTQ youth to build self-confidence, develop critical life skills, and engage their peers and community through service and advocacy.

—KD Casey

Content notes: Discussions of ghosts/death and some suspenseful elements, as well as discussion of body image/weight, depression/anxiety/compulsive behaviors, and homophobia that do not involve the use of slurs. These stories are for 18+ audiences.

UNWRITTEN RUNES

1

D'Spara's text comes early in the morning when night is still clinging to the dawn like a ghost. Zach slept, for once, insulated by the rush of water in the nearby river and the sigils drawn over the door. He'll have to scrub them off when he moves—a familiar ritual of taking a Magic Eraser to the walls. Some days, he's half-tempted to leave honest product reviews on retailers' websites. *Great for removing protective inscriptions when you get evicted or have to jump town.*

He expected to be woken as he is most days: by the flickering image of someone who died, a ghost like a hologram, its hand outstretched. Because, even with the sigils, they can slide in like smoke from under the doors, to hold out grasping palms and pitying complaints.

Today the only complaints are from D'Spara asking why Zach hasn't answered his texts like it's not six in the morning. A demand for Zach's presence at the safehouse D'Spara has across town. And ghosts are annoying, demanding, infuriating, but maybe none as annoying, demanding, or infuriating as Maryland drivers during rush hour, so Zach hustles to get ready so he can be on the road before traffic hits.

He shoves his body into clothes, his feet into his well-worn boots, his hearing aid into his ear. It squeaks as it adjusts to the ambient noise. A different squeak than the perpetual hum of ghosts. He also shoves a piece of buttered toast in his mouth, crumbs of which immediately fall below his shirt collar, leaving him itchy. At least they're a reminder that he's awake and not still dreaming, or worse.

His body aches from his last job. From getting tossed down the stairs, a set of collisions that left welts on his back and a dent in his already dented bank account from yet another visit to urgent care. He's there enough that the nurses call him *hun* in Baltimore accents thick enough to be spreadable, who probably think he's mixed up in something he shouldn't be. Which is true.

The drive to D'Spara's is predictably clogged by office workers trying to beat the rush. Even in the early morning in the full tilt of the diesel-fumed city, ghosts hover. Zach ignores them as he tries to follow his GPS's turn-by-turn directions around each traffic snarl, as he stops at a drive-thru for coffee, having to shout his order twice into the garbled speaker and just saying "That's fine" when they repeat his order back to him in an uninterpretable buzz. He asked for a coffee, large, black, a few packets of sugar, and gets a caramel latte—*fine*—made with real milk—*less fine*. It does nothing to alleviate the slight gurgle in his gut at D'Spara's summons and lack of details. Because they've been working together long enough that Zach knows the less D'Spara says about an assignment, the worse it's likely to be.

When he gets to D'Spara's, after verifying that he's who he says he is, after submitting his actual thumb print and a voice print to prove he's not possessed—*I could still be sleeping, so just let me in*—he's admitted to the safehouse. Well, he begins the slow process of admittance, the peel of one iron gate admitting him to a small anteroom, still barred by another gate. An airlock system that leaves Zach momentarily claustrophobic when both gates are closed. The low ceiling makes him hunch. He keeps his shoulders away from the walls, all studded with iron nails, and counts the time until the second gate opens enough for him to push into the safehouse.

It's dark when he gets inside. Boards cover the iron-barred windows to keep ghosts from smashing out the glass. D'Spara's sitting at a square table lit by an LED lantern, bulk impressive on a rickety kitchen chair. It takes a second to realize he's not alone.

A man probably around Zach's age is sitting in the other chair. He has a cup of coffee in front of him, another in front of D'Spara. A third in a disposable cup. And D'Spara has given Zach a lot of things over the years—assignments, reading materials, headaches, grief—but never a cup of coffee, so whoever the guy is, he must have brought it. It's hard to make out his features in the low lighting. He's broad in the shoulders with light brown hair and glasses that reflect the lantern light. Not a pro, then, because every ghost hunter Zach's ever worked with who needed vision correction switched to contacts the first time a ghost crushed their glasses. The same way Zach went to a less-effective in-ear hearing aid the first time a ghost tried to yank off his over-the-ear model.

Despite the glasses, the guy's dressed like a hunter—or would be if his clothes didn't look slightly too new, his expression a little too eager.

D'Spara makes a noise approximating a greeting, a huff

of irritation from below his graying walrus mustache that says Zach took too long in hauling himself across town, then kicks at the third empty chair with the coffee cup in front of it, an order for Zach to sit.

Zach does, folding himself onto the chair, his knees knocking against the underside of the table. The coffee cup is still warm so they can't have been waiting long, despite the irritated twitch of D'Spara's mustache.

"What's in this?" he asks, before drinking.

"Coffee." The guy slides a couple of sugar packets across as well as a few squat containers of artificial creamer. And Zach's not really in the habit of taking beverages from strangers, even ones D'Spara trusts enough to bring here, until he notices a printed-out Starbucks label sealing the lid to the cup like the guy anticipated Zach's wariness.

It takes some doing to get the label off, to doctor the coffee with two packets of sugar and a dash of Coffee-Mate. Despite his urgency in getting Zach here, D'Spara doesn't say anything and neither does the guy.

The stranger watches, though, as Zach shakes sugar packets and peels back the foil on the creamer. He has tanned skin, brown, deep-set eyes fringed with heavy lashes, and the look of someone who's never been in a fight—physical or psychically—hands unscarred on the tabletop. His nails, which are painted black, don't have so much as a chip. And D'Spara is in the habit of picking up strays, Zach among them, but usually not ones this green at the edges. A *rookie*.

Zach takes a sip of coffee.

"Temperature okay?" the guy asks. He has a flat midwestern accent, a voice deep enough to rumble.

"Coffee's good. Thanks," Zach says and the guy gets a slightly pleased smile.

D'Spara clears his throat. "Glasser, Morales. Morales, Glasser."

"Eugenio," the guy clarifies, with a slight eyeroll like this isn't the first time he's asked D'Spara to call him that.

D'Spara gives one of his sighs. "Morales is looking to join the organization." And there's an unstated *except* in there, or else he'd probably already be working for D'Spara. "Specializes in arcana."

Which definitely means Morales—*Eugenio*—is probably interested in ghost-hunting in theory. Like theory matters when a spirit is tossing you across a room.

"Glasser, I felt he could benefit from your expertise." A D'Spara way of saying Zach's being ordered to do something he doesn't want to do. Probably letting Eugenio come on a ride-along so that Zach has to babysit him while he evicts ghosts. He's gearing up to say that he can't, because, whoops, look at that, his schedule is totally full, when D'Spara slides a small manilla envelope the size of a house key across the table. "Morales is having some vision issues. I told him you'd help solve those for him."

And *fuck* that can only mean one thing. "You really think that's a good idea?" Zach asks.

Eugenio's jaw goes slightly tight, tension accentuating the tendons in his neck. "It's not something I'm asking for lightly." Like he made a pros and cons list about *learning to see ghosts* and decided that this was for him. The way he probably selected whatever college he went to.

Zach sets his coffee on the table. The chair's legs give a grind of complaint against the hard concrete floor as Zach stands. "Find someone else."

"You want to go back to freelance work?" A threat D'Spara makes every time Zach says no to something. That Zach would go back to doing odd jobs in the hopes of some compensation, with no backup. "Wouldn't want a repeat of last time."

The last time—when Zach barely scraped himself off a floor, when he drove himself to the ER, almost bleeding out. When doctors said he was lucky to have made it all. Even if, strictly speaking, he didn't. A choice that isn't one. Zach slaps his hand on the tabletop, palming the key.

"Take a week," D'Spara says. "Cabin's stocked. There's money for groceries."

Like a hundred bucks is going to begin to cover the cost. "Just so we're clear, this isn't a good idea," Zach says, then looks at Eugenio. "Be ready to go by three. We need to be there before nightfall."

WHEN ZACH RETURNS MIDAFTERNOON HAULING A DUFFEL BAG of clothes, another of gear, and a headful of doubts about why this won't work, Eugenio's waiting outside. Eugenio's still in his faux-hunting clothes—jeans, boots, a flannel that looks somehow ironed. It's rolled to the elbows, revealing his forearms, which are at least thick with muscle. Standing, he's not particularly tall, certainly shorter than one of the high boxwood shrubs around the safehouse, but broader than Zach, whose mother is always on him to eat more.

Eugenio smiles when Zach pulls up. He has a suitcase, an honest-to-god hard-sided thing with wheels more suited to business travel, like he's never had to shove a strap over his shoulder and flee. He hefts it into the trunk of Zach's Jeep, asking if he can rearrange the duffels.

"Do whatever," Zach says.

Something about it makes Eugenio laugh.

He levers himself into Zach's passenger seat, shutting the

door and buckling his seatbelt without prompting. He smells like soap or cologne, not particularly strongly, but enough to seem out of place in Zach's semi-dusty truck. He's also clearly keyed up, hands rapping against his thighs, like he's impatient to get going.

"Before we go," Zach says, "a couple ground rules."

Eugenio's eyebrows rise above the frames of his glasses.

And Zach rehearsed these on the drive over, the traffic mercifully sparce, even if Zach wished for a dumb accident or just a rubbernecking slow-down to keep him from having to do this. "This is probably going to end badly."

Eugenio smiles at that, about to say something, and Zach has to look at people as they're talking to compensate for the hearing loss in his left ear, the fade out of noise that started when he was a kid and has only grown worse as he's gotten older. Has to look at the curve of Eugenio's mouth to see the shape of his words. Which wouldn't exactly be a hardship if they weren't meeting under these circumstances.

"Mandatory pessimism." Eugenio smirks. "Got it."

"Second rule"—though there really wasn't a first—"listen when I tell you to do something." And Zach expects a bristling argument, or maybe a vigorous agreement like a class suck-up. But he gets a thoughtful nod, an incline of Eugenio's head.

"That includes if I tell you to run," Zach says. "Or to get in the truck and drive away."

That gets more of a reaction, a questioning look across the truck like Eugenio's just now realizing what he's gotten himself into.

Go back to the library, Zach thinks. They need library people, ones who can do the pages of dull research that boil down to a post-it of instructions: Go here. Kill this. Report back covered in bruises and ectoplasm. Repeat until your body can't do it any longer. Or turn into guys like D'Spara, calling the shots from the paranoid comfort of a safehouse. His derision must show.

Or possibly not, because Eugenio smiles. "You should work on that."

Zach lifts an eyebrow.

"The 'this could be dangerous' stuff." Eugenio wiggles his fingers a little sarcastically.

"It could be dangerous." Zach shakes his head. "It *is* dangerous. Don't know why you'd want to do this if you have other options."

"And yet, here I am." Eugenio doesn't say anything else, doesn't unclip his seatbelt or bail out onto the sidewalk. A stubbornness that will probably get him hurt. Might get him killed. But Zach isn't left with many other options—any, actually. And isn't that just his life? So he puts the truck in gear.

It should be a ninety-minute drive. Of course, the delay Zach was hoping for materializes and leaves them stuck on the Baltimore beltway for longer than necessary, then a slow roadwork-induced crawl on the interstate. Eugenio is a mostly quiet passenger. But he's clearly bored and he reaches to turn on the radio before Zach shakes him off.

"Makes the directions hard for me to hear," Zach says. This part is always his least favorite: the explanation part. Asking for other people to change how they talk with him, how much noise is in the room, to be aware that he can't hear very well in restaurants, truck stops, echoing cabins. Or the joking irony that Zach can't hear—except for ghosts, who he can't *not* hear. "I have moderate hearing loss in my left ear. I wear a hearing aid." There, said like it's no more remarkable than the weather, even if his hands tighten on the steering wheel.

Eugenio absorbs that. For a second, Zach thinks he's not going to respond. Which would be worse—sitting in a pitying silence.

"What's the best way for me to communicate?" Eugenio asks. Gratifyingly, he doesn't raise his voice or speak any differently from how he has been.

"It helps if we're facing each other."

Eugenio smiles at that. "Got it."

"And don't put your hand in front of your face while you're talking."

Eugenio puts his hands on his knees. He has tattoos, a few ordinary ones revealed by his sleeves, and one that looks different every time Zach looks at it. Not that Zach's been looking at his forearms. One of his wrists is encased in a battered leather cuff, its wear at odds with the rest of his store-bought appearance. "OK."

"If there's a lot of ambient noise or whatever, I probably won't be able to hear you."

"Like ghosts?"

Not like with ghosts. Because Zach can hear ghosts, always, even in his deaf ear. Something that confuses audiologists and psychologists and almost everyone he mentions it to. How the sound is different from traffic or the radio or Eugenio, who's lightly tapping his fingers against his legs.

"Like at rest stops," Zach says. Which reminds him that they need to stop for groceries. "Can you see where the nearest supermarket is?"

Eugenio smiles at that, like it's a privilege to be asked to find a Walmart Supercenter. "We should make a list." As if he can sense that Zach's main method of going to the supermarket is wandering the frozen foods aisle, shoving the things that look the least gross into his cart.

Zach lets out an exhale dramatic enough to make Eugenio laugh.

"Not big on cooking?" Eugenio asks.

"Don't really have the time." Or the patience, or the cookware, beyond the dented set he carries with him between crappy apartments. Or anyone else to cook for. If he gets truly hard up for a meal, he can go out to Pikesville and have his mom feed him enough for an entire week while fussing that he's too skinny.

"Let me see if I can change your mind."

And Zach heard him just fine in the otherwise quiet car, but if he glances over to see Eugenio's faint smirk, the stubborn push of his lower lip, well, hopefully he can blame it on the roar of traffic around them.

When Zach went to bed last night—collapsed, more accurately, face first into a mattress—he didn't think his day was going to include making a slow circuit through the produce aisle in a western Maryland Walmart with a guy he just met who apparently has a lot of opinions about citrus. And who insists on pushing the cart.

Eugenio did in fact make a list, a slow interrogation of foods Zach did and didn't like, one that involved his slight disbelieving glances when Zach said he'd eat whatever, like being semi-apathetic toward food was a moral failing.

"OK, but what do you *like*?"

And Eugenio tapped on his phone when Zach said, "Chicken, I guess," like this is a vacation and not a likely suicide mission that Zach got cornered into.

Now he's inspecting lemons, holding each up and turning it skeptically.

"We only have a hundred bucks," Zach says. Most of which is probably already spent on the bread, eggs, coffee, *ingredients*, that Eugenio piled into the cart.

Eugenio aims his chin at the sign advertising lemons as two for a dollar. "How much do you think lemons are?"

"Lemons are, I don't know—what are you even using lemons for?"

"Flavor is never a bad thing," Eugenio counters, and Zach is about to say something else when another shopper —an elderly man who smells like he needs a shower— shoves past, muttering about them clogging the aisle.

Zach is about to take it as regular annoyance, as perhaps borderline but not particularly unexpected homophobia, when he realizes he heard the guy out of his left ear. The one in which his hearing aid is turned off to deal with some of the store noise, since it picks up on whatever's loudest in the room.

"Hold still," Zach says.

Eugenio raises his eyebrows, but, to his credit, goes statue stiff.

The man—the *ghost*—lingers. He's rooting through a display, selecting and returning oranges as if inspecting them for mold. Or trying to, but each swoop of his hand comes up empty, each return a sulfurous blur. Now that Zach knows what he is, the signs are there: a flickering edge to his appearance, a certain weightlessness, a muttering like the creak of a chain in a thunderstorm. Eugenio follows his gaze, a slow turning of his head like knows something's there, even if he's looking at slightly the wrong spot.

Ghost? he mouths.

Zach nods.

At least the ghost is more or less minding his own business. And Zach's cleared ghosts out of apartments, businesses, abandoned buildings, schools, and synagogues, but there's something a little depressing about the prospect of spending eternity in a western Maryland Walmart.

He left most of his stuff in the truck, save the amulet decorating his keychain that dissuades the evil eye, and a dashed-out illustration of a sigil on a bar napkin tucked in his wallet like an old phone number. Morgan did it, that night they spent rousting ghosts from an old arcade somewhere in upstate New York, and Zach's heard a lot of ghosts plead their unfinished business but perhaps none sadder than the teenager who just wanted to exchange a fistful of printed-out tickets for a stuffed teddy bear. It'd been—well, it'd been a hard day. One made better when Morgan fed him whiskey and put him to bed in a cheap motel and slept in the bed next to his, her snores a comfort in the pale dark.

"What should we do?" Eugenio whispers. He's not loud. Or he's not loud to Zach, though the ghost stops his orange inspection to flick a look their way.

"Nothing," Zach says. "Just leave it."

Eugenio looks like he wants to argue. He has a dim aura, a limn of red around him like an indicator light. Easy to ignore. Except it flares now, slightly, anger or something else. "Won't it be stuck here?"

It will be, but there's no avoiding that. And Zach's certainly not going to clear a ghost out of here with civilians, including Eugenio, around. The man isn't malevolent as far as Zach can tell. Maybe he's recently dead, still unaware that he isn't just on the world's longest shopping trip. Maybe his world has narrowed to aisles one through four and that suits him okay. Or he could be the type to bottle all his anger, to unleash whatever supernatural torment he's holding back on the first hunter who comes calling. Who might pick Zach up and fling him and leave him gasping and then start picking off shoppers. Calculations Zach can't explain, not with their cart half full of groceries that Eugenio is checking off from a list on his phone.

Other shoppers are beginning to notice they haven't moved. A woman with her toddler sitting in the cart, the little girl's legs joyfully kicking, clears her throat. A semi-polite "Are you all done here?" that might be because they're getting clocked as a couple or might just be because they're blocking the lemon display.

The ghost, at least, shimmers like the afterimage on a video tape, a harmless bit of static, and disappears. Zach exhales, then moves the cart.

When they're done shopping—when Eugenio has managed groceries that total to seventy dollars and vastly outweigh what Zach would have gotten, enough for Zach to get a box of kosher salt and a few tall, glass-walled votives, just in case—Zach loads the groceries into the back seat of his truck. Eugenio hands him things, with various warnings that certain bags contain eggs, to not crush the bread. There's a domestic carefulness to it that Zach doesn't examine, having only known each other for all of eight hours.

"I forgot something," Eugenio says. "I'll be back in a second."

"Do not go in there and try to clear a ghost. Not by yourself. Not without... if this whole thing works, we can get him on the way back." And Zach definitely feels like a hassled parent on a road trip or one of his coaches from little league growing up, before he gave up baseball when ghosts started showing up in the stands.

Eugenio smiles at him, a broad, sheepish smile. It's far enough into the afternoon that the light's beginning to fade, the weather tipping from autumnal to chilly. His eyes look particularly bright behind his thick-lensed glasses, his mouth amused. Not that Zach is watching him speak for reasons beyond comprehension. Because they're about to spend a week in literal close quarters, and Zach shouldn't. *Can't.* For any number of reasons.

"I wasn't," Eugenio says. "I promise." He pulls the spare thirty bucks from his pocket, handing it to Zach. "Though, hypothetically, if I was going to get some ice cream, what flavor would you like?"

Which isn't exactly the question Zach was expecting. "I, uh, can't eat ice cream. Lactose intolerant."

Eugenio nods. "But you're not opposed to the idea of desserts, hypothetically?"

Zach tries to remember the last time someone asked him about his preference for really... any of this. "Hypothetically? Uh, no." He eyes the sky, which is darkening. They still have another forty minutes until they make the cabin, and despite D'Spara's assurances that it's locked up as tight as he can make it, Zach still needs to check its security. "We don't really have a lot of time."

And Eugenio leaves him with a squeeze to his arm and a promise he won't be more than five minutes.

Four and a half minutes later, Eugenio climbs into the truck with a shopping bag, the contents of which he conceals from Zach. "We should get a move on," he says, like he isn't the cause of their delay. He fidgets, enough to send his aura flickering, enough that the red film of energy clinging to him dims for a second, revealing a tattoo that's definitely in a different shape than when they were in the store.

"You all set?" Zach asks unnecessarily.

"Eager to get there?"

"Eager to get this over with." Zach tries for snappish, for put-upon. But maybe he's tired from an incomplete night's sleep or maybe it's just difficult to be mad in a parking lot at a guy who asked him what flavors of ice cream he wanted to eat, even if this entire situation makes his stomach churn. The engine makes a few coughing rotations when he flips the key like it knows this is a bad idea. But it catches, eventually, and Zach drives toward whatever the next week holds for them.

2

———

THE CABIN IS OFF A ROAD, OFF ANOTHER ROAD, OFF A THIRD road, off the highway. Even with the volume all the way up on his phone and the directions displayed as text, Zach drives slowly. Western Maryland is pretty, or would be, if Zach wasn't wondering how far the cabin is from the nearest cemetery or Civil War battlefield, about the howl of the countryside when the sun goes down. It's dusk when they arrive. Without streetlights, the woods seem to hold more of the darkness. He was raised in the suburbs, and he's used to city ghosts, who are chattier, less gruesome. Who knows what's out there watching them?

When they pull up the gravel driveway to the cabin, Eugenio hops out, stretching. "I miss being out here. Air smells different."

He's not wrong: It smells like the woods, like woodsmoke and clean dirt and ghosts who'll be knocking at the windows soon. "Unload the groceries," Zach says. "I'm going to check the perimeter."

"Maybe I should come with you."

Zach looks at the rapidly sinking sun, the prospect of

being outside of an iron-bolted door before dark. At least in the city there's light, noise, music, people, all things ghosts aren't terribly fond of. Out here there's just the two of them, Zach an unwilling beacon. "Tomorrow I'll show you the setup," he says. If they make it that far.

"I need the keys," Eugenio reminds him, so Zach fumbles open the door, turning each lock, then waiting, in case D'Spara installed some kind of alarm he didn't mention. Nothing, just the slightly musty odor of an unused house.

The cabin is nicer than Zach expected. Four small rooms: a galley-style kitchen, a living room with a sagging plaid couch, a dining room with both a regular table and a scrying table. And a sleeping area with a bed. Only one bed.

"Guess we'll flip for the couch," Eugenio says.

"Let me go check the perimeter."

Inspecting the cabin's exterior is easier than confronting what they're supposed to do over the next week. D'Spara is predictably paranoid, paranoia that's sometimes a hassle but is now reassuring. It's not even fully dark yet, but there's already howling from the nearby woods. The map said there was a river close by. Usually spirits avoid running water, lest they get swept along in currents. But either the map lied or there's an unusually high concentration of ghosts because Zach's already starting to get a headache.

There's nothing to be done about that, so he checks the cabin's façade for loose boards, hammering at the vent covers to make sure they don't admit anything bigger than a gnat. The iron-barred windows resist his effort to yank them out. The stashes of ritual objects stuck in the dirt at each of the cabin's four corners—feathers, rocks, a set of parchment scrolls encased in leather—look newly refreshed. As much as Zach could ask for since he can't ask to be excused from this whole exercise.

They topped up the gas tank at a service station right as they exited the highway. At least if they need to flee—if *Eugenio* needs to flee—he won't have to worry about that.

Zach does another rotation around the cabin, thorough enough to admit that he's probably fussing. He's been out long enough that there's the clap of the cabin's front door.

Eugenio, on the small screened-in porch covered by a slightly decayed roof. The click of a cigarette lighter and the long blow of smoke.

Zach could go in, get settled. Unpack. Plan. Except he can't leave Eugenio to whatever's lurking in the woods.

Eugenio is quiet as he smokes, taking the kind of deep sucking inhales particular to someone with broad shoulders. "Sorry that you got forced into this," he says after a few minutes. Like he isn't responsible for Zach being here.

Zach makes a noise that he hopes encapsulates his annoyance at the situation. Though it's hard to be annoyed in the autumn cool, with Eugenio letting out smokey exhales that blend with the mist around them. He's wearing a Henley. He pushes its sleeves up even further to reveal the symbols Zach only caught glimpses of earlier. Tattoos, moving ones, shapes running under his skin like water. Protection symbols and abstract shapes that move slickly, an ever-changing inkblot.

Eugenio must see him looking at them; he rotates his wrist as if showing them off. The muscles in his forearm ripple, patterns shaping and unshaping. "They're a barometer. Kind of. They'll tell me if there's something malevolent around. I'm surprised you don't have 'em."

"My parents wouldn't like those very much."

Eugenio raises his eyebrows in question.

"Jewish parents. They can accept that I have a degree in the occult"— which, he does, though only a master's and he gets no end of grief from them for it not being a doctorate— "but tattoos wouldn't exactly go over well at shul."

Eugenio laughs at that, not meanly. "Yeah, my folks don't love that this is what I'm doing. I mean, they don't really believe in all this stuff." He motions to the cabin, the field, the woods vibrating with spirits.

"Atheists?"

Eugenio shakes his head. "Not quite. Religious studies professors. Arcana is supposed to be something you get off interlibrary loan. This is a little too hands-on for their taste." He grinds his cigarette into the side of a metal trash can. "Speaking of, did you want to get started?"

What Zach wants is a nap, maybe, or some dinner and a nap. Or some dinner and not to have an argument about which of them is getting the bed, and to be left alone. To be back in his crappy Baltimore apartment with some takeout, a movie, nothing joining him in the dark but the flickers of the TV. "Sure," he says. Or possibly sighs.

Eugenio's mouth edges up at the corner. "I got some food started, if you want to wait until after we eat."

He opens the cabin door and sure enough, smells begin to waft out of it—the familiar scent of chicken and a few other things Zach can't place. It eases some of the resentful churning in his gut.

"After dinner works." And if Zach wasn't sure he was imagining it, he'd think Eugenio's tattoos somehow look pleased.

Dinner turns out to be chicken, a set of foil-wrapped baked potatoes, and an honest-to-god-salad. It's *good*, and he must say it a few times, because Eugenio's smile is deep enough to reveal a dimple in his cheek.

"Figured it was the least I could do." Eugenio clears away the chicken, promising to turn the leftovers into something else. A purposeful clatter emerges from the kitchen. Zach might have had his entire week derailed by this whole exercise but he can also hear his mother's voice telling him to get up and go be helpful.

He finds Eugenio collecting chicken fat from the pan into a container. And it's familiar enough to what Zach's family does that something in his chest aches. *I hope he doesn't die doing something stupid.* With it, *I hope I don't get him killed.*

"Everything good?' Eugenio asks.

And Zach nods and mumbles something about needing to get set up.

Eugenio is predictably eager. Overeager. His face falls a little when Zach says they should ease into scrying via the fundamentals.

"You think D'Spara would really take me on if I didn't know those?" Eugenio asks.

He's probably right, but Zach also doesn't want to rush things before he gets a sense of how Eugenio works magic. "He hasn't taken you on, yet."

With that, the tilt of Eugenio's chin, the subtle flare of his nostrils. "He will."

"Not without my say so." Or at the very least a clear demonstration that Eugenio can more-or-less do whatever magic D'Spara demands.

Eugenio looks like he's going to say something but thinks better of it, then begins rummaging in his bag.

Zach expected books, maybe, or cards. Overly complicated numerology. An academic's approach to magic.

Instead Eugenio produces a bag of earth. He pauses before he dumps some of it onto the scarred table surface, recently cleared of their dishes. "We could use the other table." The scrying table, which is leaning against the wall, its wings folded down.

"Nice try," Zach says, and Eugenio's laugh is loud against the cabin walls.

His laugh, then an echo, one inaudible to human—most human—ears. A hum of ghosts like the howl of the wind, bypassing Zach's outer ear in favor of going directly into his brain. He tightens his hands against the tabletop, apparently enough to draw Eugenio's attention.

"Ghosts?" he asks, the same way he did in Walmart, though with an edge of fear like he's just realizing it's the two of them out here alone against the darkness.

"There's always ghosts." And it's a good thing Zach isn't trying to be reassuring, because he clearly isn't.

Eugenio's jaw goes tense, different than when he was just being stubborn.

"Hunting isn't for everyone," Zach continues. An understatement. Because half the guys who he's worked with end up on the wrong side of the grave. "There's other kinds of magic."

"Not to me." Though Eugenio doesn't offer anything else by way of explanation. He spills out the dirt, forming it into neat rows like agricultural furrows. Except instead of using his hand, he directs it with a flick in his wrist and several flares of red, outcroppings from his aura. It's smooth. Practiced. Maybe overly so, form precise. So not an amateur, then. Worse. A perfectionist.

After a few minutes, he looks back up at Zach in question. A *see, I told you so* expression. His eyes are bright behind his glasses, shoulders set like he's rising to a physical challenge, and Zach should be eager to just get all of this done with. That whatever conclusion they'll come to—

death, injury, the improbability of success—at least gets achieved quickly. No sense in dragging this out. No sense in this being anything but business. Because it's not.

An instinct counterbalanced by Eugenio's smile, like this should be *fun*.

"OK, you can do a little object rearrangement," Zach says.

Eugenio gives a huff of disbelief.

"That all you got?"

"No."

"So impress me."

And Eugenio's smile goes impossibly deeper.

THEY'RE AT IT FOR LONGER THAN ZACH INTENDS, ENOUGH that the cabin goes the particular kind of dark exclusive to the woods, night like a palpable thing sitting on their shoulders, only brightened by the yellow cabin lighting. Eugenio is easy to rile, eager to impress, the red glow of his aura flickering as he moves through various types of magic. He's stuck mostly to physical effects—conjuring and transmutations— but he was right to be confident-bordering-on-cocky about his skills. He's *good*. That might make this whole thing even worse. Because Zach could refuse if Eugenio didn't have the requisite knowhow. But he does. So Zach can't.

Eventually Eugenio yawns expansively.

"Tired?" Zach asks. Possibly goads. Though he is too.

Eugenio returns the dirt to its carrying bag with a brush of his cupped hand. "The couch is calling my name."

"I thought we were going to flip for it."

"You look like you need a little more legroom than I do." Accompanied by a once-over, like Zach somehow hasn't noticed the difference in their heights. "Besides, that took enough out of me I should be able to sleep anywhere. Even that couch." He gives its arm a tap and only winces slightly when it produces a puff of dust.

Zach's travelled with a lot of hunters. That's the nature of the business. Sharing living space, especially temporary living space, is just part and parcel with it. Hell, he's sewn up people whose names he forgot a week later, shared no-name hotel beds with people he never saw again, hoping they caught common sense and quit.

It's nothing to have Eugenio strip down in the living room. Nothing to have him tug off his Henley, which he folds before putting it back into his suitcase. And Zach doesn't watch him, and doesn't not watch him, not the drag of the fabric over his shoulders or the flex of muscles in his back as he roots around in bag.

"Let me go see if there's another blanket," Zach says. Because this place might be sealed up tight against spiritual trespassers, but it probably isn't heated for shit.

He busies himself with that, with shaking out various blankets and setting up the bed. He brushes his teeth and takes out his hearing aid. Even around Morgan and other hunters he knows well, he doesn't like having it out. The woods are, at least, mostly quiet of everything save cricket song and the haunting call of owls, though there's a breathless whisper under them, a murmur of the dead.

It shouldn't bother him. It's been happening since he young, too young to know what they were. Since his parents made overjoyed faces when he said he was hearing things in his deaf ear. Ones that only lasted for the trip to the audiologist, that slowly transitioned to horror when he said he wasn't just hearing things, but *voices*.

He's broken from his contemplation of the old but clean

sheets, the faded but relatively dust-free bedspread, by Eugenio, who waits until Zach can see him before asking if he's done in the bathroom.

He's changed into sweats, a T-shirt that sits close to his body. He hasn't taken off the battered leather cuff at his wrist. Either he catches Zach looking or the cuff itself itches, because he rubs his fingers under it. The surrounding tattoos are as sleepy as he looks, waving softly.

"You need anything?" Zach asks, meaning to say *something*. To find the remnants of his own irritation.

Eugenio smiles, shakes his head. His glasses reflect the bedside lamp. "Just to see a ghost."

Zach should tell him that it doesn't work like that—that some people have the sight and some don't, and that's just the way of things. "Maybe tomorrow. Rest up."

And Eugenio looks far too pleased at that for someone who's about to sleep on a couch made mostly of springs.

3

Things Eugenio is apparently not: A seer. A light sleeper. A morning person. The second two conspire to keep him on the couch, after Zach spends longer than he should have sleeping in. It's mid-morning, the sun burning the mist away. With it, whatever ghosts might come to interrupt his dreams. A good night's sleep, except for how he woke up cold, in a bed that wasn't objectively that big but felt empty. He dreamed, which wasn't unusual, though his dreams are normally closer to nightmares, memories from bad hunts amplified, a long fall into nothingness like that time when—

These weren't those.

And he's grateful that Eugenio is sleeping soundly when he goes to shower off the remnants.

Eugenio brought coffee, a bag of the stuff that's too expensive to have been bought at the Walmart. Zach measures out a few scoops into a filter, coaxes water from the gurgling kitchen sink. Brews coffee and watches it drip with the same domestic feeling he couldn't shake from the day before. That this might work out okay.

Or would, if he didn't see a figure out the window,

making its way across a sea of grass. Almost invisible in the morning sunlight. It's moving in that stutter-stop way ghosts have but with no particular urgency. Still. A reminder of why they're here. That this is business. That it can't be anything other than that.

He pours two mugs of coffee, dosing one with soy milk and leaving the other black. Eugenio's still asleep on the couch, a blanket wrapped around him. His legs are folded, his shoulders hunched. The couch springs give a complaining squeak as he shifts. They could both fit in the bed, probably. Definitely. Without much maneuvering. Zach's shared with other people over the years. It's surprising how many times you pull into a shitty motel to find they're out of double rooms. Eugenio is a stranger, still, though one who blinks awake when Zach shakes him by the ankle, who pats the end table looking for his glasses, his eyelashes magnified by the lenses.

"I made coffee," Zach says. "I wasn't sure how you took it."

"Sweet."

And it takes Zach a second to realize he's requesting sugar.

He finds a box of sugar packets in a back cabinet, old but fine, and hands two to Eugenio, who lays out his palm requesting two more. So not just sweet, but practically syrup, and it's a strange thing to know about someone he met all of thirty hours ago.

Over the course of the morning, he learns that Eugenio is pretty much nonverbal until he's had his first long, groaning sip of coffee. With it, a morning cigarette, an apology for knowing it's a bad habit. Though he looks like he's bordering on cozy, wrapped in sweatpants and a too large sweatshirt. He catches Zach looking because he just shrugs and says, "My ex left it when he left," simple as that. Except it makes things slightly more complicated.

He also learns that Eugenio both can cook and likes to, humming as he makes breakfast, and going slightly pink from the heat in the kitchen or Zach's third *This is really good*, though his smile dims a little when Zach says, "Like twice as good as Hot Pockets," mostly to wind him up.

"We gonna do some scrying today?" Eugenio says, after they've eaten and Zach's rinsed the dishes.

And Zach should say no. Should say they can wait until tomorrow. Should tell Eugenio that he's sorry, but he just can't do this. That he'll buy him a box of Nicorette and give him a ride back to Baltimore, both things that might extend his chances of survival. Except a text comes in from D'Spara, checking in, a single ? that makes Zach want to throw his phone in a nearby river.

He could tell D'Spara to fuck off. Except the last time he tried to strike out on his own, D'Spara was outside the ER when Zach limped out. He'd bought Zach a sandwich and, over pit beef, told Zach that this job would kill him if he let it, and Zach almost said *It already has.*

"Sure," Zach says, regretting it as soon as he says it.

It must show because Eugenio smiles and claps him on the arm. "I'm a quick study. You'll see."

And Zach doesn't tell him that's what he's worried about.

THEY'VE ONLY BEEN AT THE SCRYING TABLE FOR A FEW minutes, but it only takes a few minutes to realize what Eugenio is doing wrong in scrying—pretty much everything.

It's heartening in a way. Eugenio's smooth incantations

from the night before are nowhere to be found. Now his movements are stiff bordering on jagged. He jerks his palm over the sigil inlaid into the table.

He's nervous, clearly, concentrating like he's being graded on this.

He smiles when Zach says that. Less so when he adds, "There isn't a ghost-hunting honor roll."

Zach reaches for his hand, not quite making contact. "You can't keep moving your hand like that."

Eugenio shifts his palm, also incorrectly. "I'm supposed to move my hand."

"Yes, you're supposed to move your hand. Just not like *that*." And Zach's apprehension about this—that Eugenio will bring forth something that they can't control, that he'll be injured or killed—is replaced by more prosaic irritation. Because decent scrying is about moving your hand slightly, subtly, imperceptibly, enough to convince a reticent ghost that you're just here to talk and not to banish them into whatever inky blackness occupies the world beyond. And Eugenio is doing it *wrong*.

Zach could tell him that he's doing well. Lie to him and say, "Yep, go get 'em." But of course, D'Spara won't take just Zach's word for it, and Eugenio shouldn't be out hunting if he doesn't know what he's doing—and he clearly doesn't.

On top of that, Eugenio is frustrated: a lip-chewing, jaw-clenching, temple-throbbing kind of irritation. It's not that surprising. Scrying, even well-done scrying, hurts. What Eugenio is doing—throwing his energy into the room and having it reverberate back to his body—must sting. His aura pulses bright red around him. Not that Zach's been watching him. Not that his aura is, well, a pretty nice one. Hot. Temperature-wise.

It goes on like that for most of the day, with breaks for

food, for Eugenio to go take his frustration out on a pack of cigarettes. Dusk is falling when Zach calls it a day. He rechecks the perimeter, Eugenio trailing behind, eager to discuss the various charms and trinkets. He looks tired, deep circles under his eyes. The kind of tiredness Zach's seen often enough in the mirror.

"You should rest," Zach says, when they're sitting on the porch, Eugenio tapping an unlit cigarette vaguely against the arm of one of the Adirondack chairs.

Instead Eugenio exhales another sigh. "This would be a nice place to go on vacation."

It would be. Picturesque, with the mist rising from the forest, with fading greenery and the distant flow of water. If not for the spirits at the edge of the clearing, ducking in and out of the tree line. Come night, Zach expects the scratch of their fingers against the iron bars of the windows, their low demands that Zach can't block out even with a pillow over his hearing ear.

Shedim, they're called, and they move like shades now, like shadows deepening dusk into night.

Eugenio taps his cigarette again. Even that looks exhausted. His aura fades from bright to brickish red, and shit, Zach shouldn't have let him push himself like that. He needs rest, on a real bed. Probably some food. Possibly to find a different profession, one that comes with a lot of cross-referencing and no spiritual exhaustion.

"We should go inside before it gets full dark," Zach says. Eugenio follows, hovering as Zach secures the bolts for the door. Whatever excitement he had about scrying the night before has worn off, and now they're left in a cabin with nothing to do for the evening except look at each other and avoid the ghosts lurking outside.

"Go sit down." He nudges Eugenio's shoulder, hand

safely around the fabric of Eugenio's sweatshirt, away from the flicker of his tattoos. Eugenio looks like he might argue for a second, then goes, dragging himself woozily to the couch.

Zach finds a box of tea in the kitchen that smells like dried flowers and promises to be gently caffeinated. He boils water, then dumps a few sugar packets into a mug along with a tea bag. He carries it out to Eugenio, who has his feet up, shoes off. His head is tilted back like he's examining something on the ceiling.

Eugenio takes the mug, cupping it, smiling like Zach did something other than ensure that he's not going pass out.

"Is that, uh, sweet enough?" Zach asks after a minute.

"It's perfect. Thanks."

"If you tell me what to do with the food for dinner, I can probably figure it out."

Another smile. "I'll be all right. Don't love being cooped up in here all night"—and Zach wishes he'd thought to go for at least a run that morning, so that he wouldn't spend a full twenty-four hours stuck in this place—"but I'll manage."

Eugenio looks better after that mug of tea and another that Zach brews for him. The color's back in his face. He gets up, stretching to his full height, which puts his face about level with Zach's shoulder. Not that Zach is considering how they might fit together.

"I can make dinner if you want to..." Eugenio begins, then trails off. "I don't know, do whatever?"

The cabin doesn't have a TV; Zach's phone has two wavering bars of service. Zach brought books, most of which are arcana and comic trade paperbacks, none of which hold a lot of appeal. "Would it bother you if I was in the kitchen?"

"No." Eugenio smiles. "It wouldn't."

Zach doesn't watch him cook, exactly, but there's something soothing about how he moves, the efficiency of his hands around the handle of a knife. The way he does everything with intentionality. He's humming again, a normal hum against the louder background of the woods—crickets and night-flying birds and the increasing howl of ghosts. One gives an especially plaintive cry, a sound like icy fingers up Zach's neck.

Eugenio must see him shiver. "All good?"

"Just the wind picking up."

He gives a disbelieving hum. "That one even I could hear."

"Why do you want to see them, anyway? D'Spara needs plenty of people who can, like, do the reading for the rest of us."

"I thought you said there was no ghost-hunting honor roll."

Zach tries not to laugh and doesn't quite succeed. And doesn't quite succeed in not watching the brightening flush to Eugenio's cheeks or the pleased look he gets when he goes back to turning leftovers into dinner.

They eat, at the normal table, the scrying one already packed up. Chicken pasta that somehow feels fancier than its constituent ingredients.

Zach might be making appreciative noises, possibly too many of them, because Eugenio asks, "When was the last time someone cooked for you?"

"Outside of my family? Not sure. Sometimes on jobs, I guess." Which does happen, out of necessity or occasional gratitude that Zach removed a marauding ghost from someone's house.

Eugenio makes an assessing hum. "Must be hard, if you're traveling all the time."

Zach's parents have said the same thing, along with Morgan, who tells him to work less and to take care of himself more. Perhaps not with an edge to it, or a question that Zach doesn't quite know what to do with. Except to say that it's hard, scraping himself up off whatever floor ghosts have tossed him onto, trying to piece together enough to afford rent and gas money. How his family fusses at him to take time off, as if ghosts take time off from him. How he wakes most mornings to fading figures at the foot of his bed, a thousand pleading requests he doesn't know how to answer.

"It is." His voice is hoarse. He tries to wash the lingering feeling of dissatisfaction away with a glass of tap water.

He does the dishes after dinner, standing at the sink while Eugenio leans against the counter. An easy conversation—about Eugenio's family, about his time at college and the years after, trying to make it in the unmagical world. "You asked, before, why I want to see ghosts."

Zach's hands are still immersed in soapy water. A loose curl of hair falls across his forehead, and he shakes it back, unsuccessfully.

Eugenio raises his hand fingers, not quite making contact with Zach's skin. "Do you want me to..." And he moves the strand of hair, lightly, the air between them charged as his aura overlaps with Zach's. "I can hear them." Eugenio's voice is low, like whatever's outside might overhear. "See them sometimes like something out of the corner of my eye."

His hand is still in Zach's hair, and he withdraws it, the heat from his fingertips like sparks across Zach's face.

"I just want to have some say over it," Eugenio adds. "Make it be on purpose if I can't get rid of them."

Said without much inflection, but with an undercurrent

Zach understands, that desire to wrest control of something fundamentally uncontrollable. Something that he can't possibly refuse, even if he knows the cost. "I hear them all the time. See them too. Most days when I wake up, they're at the foot of my bed." His throat goes tight. "You should be sure this is what you want. It's not like there's a way out."

He expects apprehension, or Eugenio to withdraw to the safety of a few feet away. Maybe Zach should insist on it. That he should coat himself in cool air and rational thinking. Make that pros and cons list after all.

Instead he's met with the set of Eugenio's jaw. "This is what I want."

"Okay," Zach says.

There's a long call outside: a ghost, a bird, the wind. A reminder that they're not alone. That this trapped little bubble of safety is inherently temporary. Eugenio steps back, leaving Zach to shiver momentarily, then turn back to the dishes. "You should take the bed tonight," he says, trying to be conversational and probably failing. "Get some real rest."

"Thanks, but there's no way you're going to fit on the couch."

They'd fit together in bed. In *the* bed. A distinction Zach should be making. "You sure about sleeping there?"

"I'll be okay." With it, a stretch, a roll of Eugenio's shoulders in his sweatshirt. An eye toward the bed, and if he's looking at the whole unoccupied side, it's probably because it has marginally fewer springs.

4

EUGENIO GETS UP WHEN HE DOES THE NEXT MORNING, A HALF-sleepy grumbling that Zach has to admit is cute. Or would be, until he hovers as Zach is making coffee, giving a disapproving enough stare that Zach finally gets out of the way.

"Seems like you want to do this," Zach says, and laughs as Eugenio dumps the grounds back into the container, then remeasures them into the filter.

Coffee, a morning cigarette, a promise that there'll be breakfast if Zach wants to go out for a run. *A nice place to vacation.* Except there's scrying waiting for them both when he gets back. "Are you sure you're OK with me being gone for a while?" he asks.

Eugenio rolls his eyes fondly. "I made it to twenty-eight without you looking out for me."

And Zach laces up his running shoes and hopes they both make it to twenty-nine.

The woods are cool, brisk with morning air, with the passing shadows of spirits who part as he cuts through on a running trail. The maps weren't lying: There is a river nearby, a soothing rush of water. For a minute, he considers what it'd be like without ghosts. If he was actually on vacation, out for a run, going back to breakfast and a day spent as they chose it. Hiking slowly through the woods around here or off to explore whatever tourist-trap towns are nearby. Possibly at a restaurant that Eugenio picked, someplace with cloth napkins and low lighting. Returning to sit in Zach's Jeep and watch the field around the cabin. An anticipatory wait, then a slow lean in together, kissing just to kiss as fireflies blink in approval.

But they can't. Because the world is what it is. Because there are ghosts around every stump and hollow.

And if they see energy bridging between two people, they'll climb right up and walk it. A possession. Worse. Zach died, once, a death that didn't quite take, but nothing he'd wish on anyone. Especially not a novice ghost hunter. Especially not Eugenio, who's making him breakfast and who smiled at Zach and practically shoved him out the door. Zach doesn't want to have to tie him down. Not to extract a dybbuk.

A *can't* that shapes Zach's life. That it is easy to be alone, or to hook up and leave, for other people to do the same. A simplicity that feels markedly less simple, and Zach takes it out on the trail dirt and runs until his legs feel pleasantly sore.

Despite the morning chill, he's flushed when he gets back to the cabin, stripping his shirt and tucking it in the waistband of his running shorts. He has to slide by where Eugenio's cooking to get a glass of water, to get an assessing stare that's probably because he's sweaty in the kitchen.

"Food almost ready?" Zach asks.

Eugenio blinks a few times at him, a motion matched by the spike of his tattoos. "You hungry?"

"I could eat."

And Eugenio's answering smile sends warmth up Zach's overheated neck.

After breakfast, Zach unfolds the scrying table, bracing himself for another day of frustration.

But nothing prepares him for Eugenio not sitting in the chair across from him, but instead going to his knees.

"Um," Zach says coherently, "what're you doing?"

"I was doing some reading about how a change in perspective might help." Said innocently enough if he didn't cast a look up at Zach through his eyelashes.

"Oh, uh, makes sense."

Eugenio doesn't move for a long while, his hand skimming the tabletop like he's running his fingers over the surface of water. His eyes are closed. From this angle, the threads of his eyelashes are obvious against his cheek, his lips full from the actions of his teeth.

For someone who spends much of his time asking ghosts to kindly shuffle off into metaphysical space, Zach doesn't have much conversation with divine. He does now, praying diffusely that Eugenio gets up off his knees—and that he doesn't look too closely at Zach's lap.

It's good there aren't any ghosts here, because they'd probably point out the tendrils of Zach's energy he can't quite contain, faint blue lights that crackle from his fingertips. Because ghosts are basically mischievous cats that sometimes try to kill you and make fun of you the rest of the time.

Zach turns his head to the side, spitting three times. No use in drawing the evil eye on top of everything else.

Eugenio rises, brushing dust off his pant legs, then resettles himself at the table. He's a little too big for the chair he's occupying; it creaks slightly. "You think that was a ghost?"

But it's clear he knows it's not, and Zach rolls his eyes.

Eugenio shakes his palm out a few times like he's mentally gearing up to try again. "Okay. Here goes whatever." He wafts a palm down onto the table's surface. Nothing happens.

"Be gentle," Zach advises. "Sometimes you have to finesse it a little."

Eugenio arches an eyebrow.

"Fuck, I know, I know, that's not helpful." Zach gathers his energies, reining in the pale blue that seems to glow brighter in the dim light of the cabin. He sweeps his hand out, hovering it over one of the symbols carved in the table, clearing his mind to that particular mental space between boredom and not boredom. An open space for whatever's occupying the area around them to come have a chat.

Something flickers at the edge of his consciousness, a spirit saying hello like a long call through a valley. "Feel that?" Zach says.

"I know how to cast my aura. And you didn't even move your hand."

"I didn't need to. If I moved my hand like I was scrying, the ghost would refuse my invitation."

"They do that with me anyway."

"Then don't give 'em another reason to." There's another call, something closer, like a voice muffled by the wall of the next room. Zach lets out a curl of energy, an *I hear you, I hear you* that brings a rattling response.

"Was I supposed to see something?" Eugenio says.

"Exactly." It's a little gloating, and Eugenio doesn't throw up his hands or tell Zach to fuck off, but he probably should.

"Talk me through it." Eugenio situates his hand near

Zach's, close enough to feel his warmth. "Tell me what you're doing."

"Okay." And it's kind of strange to self-narrate. "I know the ghost is here. There's always one around—" Another rattle, this one shaking the cabin's walls. "Ghosts can see, kind of. It's like an old stereoscope viewer. Flashes and blinks. We're shadows to them, just as they are to us. So if I shift my whole body, it's harder to tell that I'm fluttering my hand over the sigil."

Another shake. A call. And Zach scoops his hand down before jerking it up. "See, that's what I don't want to do."

"Yeah, I got that. I know a hundred things I'm not supposed be doing."

"You can't force it." He reaches for Eugenio, stilling the motion of his hand before Eugenio summons something truly nasty. Their auras overlap, their auras and their finger-tips. "Sometimes you gotta do stuff by feel."

One corner of Eugenio's mouth turns up in a frustrated half-smile. His tattoos jump like the waves of a heart moni-tor. There's a charge in the air, maybe from an oncoming late afternoon thunderstorm, or their energies in contact, or how Eugenio's eyes go a little wide when Zach shifts his hand, circling Eugenio's wrist. His pulse thrums against Zach's fingers.

"Can you feel that?" Eugenio asks.

The room's atmosphere goes cloud-heavy. A sure sign of something, massive, loping, on the horizon. Dangerous. Exciting.

"Try now," Zach breathes, and Eugenio doesn't pull away from his grip as he moves his body closer, fractionally closer, aligning it with the highway of energy paving the room.

Something explodes. White. Flashing. A bang like every

door swinging open and booming shut. When Zach comes to on the tabletop, Eugenio is lying on the floor looking stunned.

And Zach shouldn't laugh. He shouldn't. He's taken energy blasts off his chest and back and shoulders. Summoning ghosts is practically a declaration of masochism, or at least, a solid reason to invest in Advil. But Eugenio looks like he's got cartoon birds flapping around his head.

After a minute, Eugenio laughs too.

"Fuck." Eugenio takes Zach's hand when he offers it up, wobbling slightly, then hauls himself over to the plaid-upholstered couch, which sags a little pitifully under his weight.

Zach sits next to him, the couch tipping them both to center. Eugenio leans half against its back, half on Zach's shoulder, breathing purposefully.

"Feels like I just stuck a fork in an outlet." Eugenio's tattoos agree, spikes and shards of ink coalescing back to normal over the next few minutes. Zach gets lost in their patterns, enough that it's startling when Eugenio moves away from him, reaching over to the end table he's been using as a nightstand for his glasses. He unfolds them, sliding them on. For a second, Zach imagines him bent studiously over a library carrel, extracting meaning from some long-forgotten tome, his hands ruffling patterns in his hair. His shoulders barely contained by whatever shirt he's wearing and...

"Sleeping on this tonight is going to be fantastic." Eugenio pats the couch a little despairingly. It offers up a little cough of dust.

"Sleep with me." And Zach doesn't need any particular extrasensory powers to register Eugenio's surprise. "I mean, there's a bed. It's not that comfortable, but it's probably better than this thing."

Eugenio's expression settles. His tattoos give what might be an anticipatory jump. "Yeah, all right." He smiles. "If you're offering."

A STORM BLOWS IN THAT NIGHT, BRINGING WITH IT THE VOICES of the dead. Whispers creep through the windows and call from under the doorjambs. Zach's head throbs. When he was a child, he'd sit in his bedroom, fingers in both ears trying to block them out. Now he knows the only solution is to ride it out, even if every change in barometric pressure brings with it a hail of spirits.

He doesn't hear Eugenio get up or boil the dented tea kettle. But there's a mug of tea set in front of him, a reassuring hand between his shoulder blades. The soft reddish presence of Eugenio's aura, smoothing out the cracks in his own.

"Is it always this bad?" Eugenio asks.

Zach shakes his head. "Usually, it's worse. Helps that we're so far from everything. Baltimore was hell in a storm like this. My parents live near a cemetery."

"I guess that's one good thing about growing up in rural Indiana." Eugenio glances around like he's checking the corners of the cabin for ghosts. "They aren't here, are they?"

Zach takes a restorative sip of tea. "You'd know if they were. It can get dramatic."

"Anything I should know if things get really bad?"

"Yeah. Get in the truck. Drive."

"You can't shake me that easily, Zach." He's said Zach's name like that a few times, like he's teasing, the kind of connection that's like a homing beacon for malevolent entities. He nudges Zach's shoulder with his own and doesn't quite move away. Zach should tell him to go sit on the couch. Maybe on the porch or in the safety of a rubber-tired vehicle. That building a bridge between them—any kind of bridge—leaves a road open for ghosts to walk. It is, for a thousand reasons, a bad idea, one that whispers to Zach the way the ghosts do. That perhaps the spirits will for once pass over him and leave him alone. That perhaps they can have something together, and drive away the darkness, if only for a little while.

He finishes his tea.

His hands are unsteady without the warmth of his mug. He rummages in his duffel, withdrawing his bag of lots, polished stones inscribed with symbols that are supposed to reveal the will of the divine, but mostly make him feel like a kid with a fidget toy. He spills them out on the tabletop.

Eugenio reaches for one, then stills.

Zach knocks a stone toward him. "You can go ahead."

Eugenio's nails are painted the same color as the stone, a metallic black. His wide leather cuff sits around his wrist; Zach gets the urge to ask what's under its strap. A dangerous thought, a spike of energy like ungrounded lightning. He breathes, shackling his aura as best he can and hoping his thoughts aren't obvious.

Eugenio doesn't seem to notice. He flips the stone across the tabletop. It lands with its symbol facing upward. He studies it, tracing the edge of the inscription with his nail. Zach swears he can feel a similar touch ghosting on the back of his palm. Another stroke of his finger. This time, there's no mistaking it: An answering brush like Eugenio touched him, higher this time, on the now-sensitized skin of his forearm. Once more, a slow, lingering trace, and Eugenio has to know what he's doing, especially as Zach shifts in his chair and finds no respite. Especially as he can sense his own energy swell, eclipsing the space between them, calling out to meet Eugenio's.

"Maybe lots are a bad idea," Zach says. "Given the, uh, storm and everything."

Eugenio smiles at that, a smile that's accompanied by another pulse of his aura, a bright coalescence aimed directly at Zach. He taps a stone with the pad of his finger. "Tell me about these."

A lesson, then, though one that might be for Zach's sake rather than his own. "A lot of people use tarot. Or the patterns of oil on water." Zach captures a stone in his palm, a familiar reassuring weight. "These always came a little easier for me."

Eugenio smiles. "Doesn't really seem like any of this comes particularly difficult for you."

"It does and it doesn't. For the first couple years, I wasn't really sure what was happening. There'd be these voices, and they all *wanted* something. I didn't know what to do. It's kind of funny, in retrospect. My parents took me to an audiologist"—he touches his fingers to the hearing aid sitting in one ear—"then a psychiatrist. It got better when they finally called up a rabbi who told them I was a yidde'oni. An interrogator of the dead."

"That must have been hard for them to take," Eugenio says.

"Made the 'I'm gay' conversation a lot easier, believe me." Well, it would have if they didn't immediately switch from setting him up with their friends' daughters to their friends' sons, who were equally skeptical of his chosen career. Job. Whatever he's doing, sitting in the Maryland woods. "By then they were happy with anything that seemed remotely tied to the world."

Eugenio laughs at that, loud. For a second the cabin is filled with that and not the calls of the dead outside. "Yeah, that must have put things in perspective. Mine were... I think it helped I gave them a bibliography when I told them I was bi. The whole chasing ghosts thing is harder to explain. It'd be easier if I could, you know, catch them."

Zach drops a hand on the table, near enough to Eugenio's that their auras overlap. Eugenio looks down at his hand, inching his pinky closer to Zach's thumb. It's warm, a different kind of warmth than mere physical heat. The tension in Zach's neck and shoulders eases. He picks up a stone. "Did you still want to try casting?"

"Sure." Eugenio holds out his hand.

Zach drops two stones into it, one with a kaf inscribed on it, the other a lamed. "C-shape for *yes*. Uh, squiggle for *no*."

"I know the Hebrew alphabet, Zach," Eugenio says. "What if they're both face up or face down?"

"Cast them again."

"We might be here for a while." Though they're in this cabin until Eugenio can summon and dismiss a ghost. Which might be a while anyway.

"You can just do one as a *yes* or *no* for face up or face down. If you're in a hurry."

Eugenio smiles at that. "Some things are worth an effort." He gathers himself, eyes closed, stones rolling in his palm, like he's collecting his energies to cast. His aura shrinks slightly, flickering a more concentrated red. But he doesn't toss them, instead opening one eye. "Should I say it out loud?"

"The stones don't need physical voice to work. If you'd, uh, prefer to keep it a secret."

Eugenio re-closes his eye, though his mouth retains an amused tilt. "Good, 'cause it's a little embarrassing."

An unstated question, one Zach can probably guess from all their frustrated hours together. "You're gonna be able to scry. It just takes some people a little longer but you'll get it."

Eugenio's smile widens. "Not what I was going to ask but appreciate the vote of confidence." He tosses the stones on the tabletop. Kaf up, lamed down. An unambiguous *yes*. "Thought so."

"You gonna tell me what you asked for?"

"It's more fun if it's a surprise." He doesn't reach for the stones again, though his palm is still curved upward toward the ceiling, a basin of warm flickering red light. A reminder of how easily Zach could slide their hands together.

One of the windowpanes rattles. A reminder of why he can't.

Zach collects the stones from the tabletop, offering them to Eugenio, who tosses them in his cupped hands like dice. "You gonna blow on them?" Eugenio asks.

"It's not a casino."

Shrugging, Eugenio casts the stones on the table. Another question. One to which he gets an ambiguous answer, both stones facing up. "Yes *and* no. Interesting."

He repeats the process again, this time holding the stones out for Zach's inspection. And Zach, on impulse, leans forward, blowing slightly, a puff of air in Eugenio's palm. He's rewarded with a flicker of Eugenio's aura, by his pleased knowing grin.

And a sharp rap at the door. Eugenio scoots back his chair, as if going to answer it.

"Don't," Zach says, tugging him back toward the table. "It's nothing. The wind."

"How do you know?"

"I'd be able to tell. People feel different."

"So whatever that is isn't people."

"It's not." Because this has the shape of a spirit, though one that's perhaps a touch more corporeal if he can sense it through the iron-bolted door.

"I have a knife," Eugenio offers.

"Can it cut through ghosts?"

He grins. "It might."

"It's fine. Just. Don't move too much. Usually they go away."

They sit for a minute, Eugenio's shoulders stiff, Zach counting down from one hundred mentally. The stones are lying on the tabletop. They begin rattling, subtly at first, Eugenio possibly tapping his foot under the table, disturbing its surface.

"Quit shaking your leg," Zach says.

"I wasn't."

"Shit." Because the clacking of the stones intensifies, along with the shiver of glass in the windows, the wind blowing in ever-greater gusts. There's not much cover in this place. They should have boarded the windows, just to be safe. Zach should have insisted on someplace even more remote. As if there was a place too remote from death. A card deck's worth of possibilities, shuffled, scattering. "If it gets bad, I meant it. Get in the Jeep. Go."

Eugenio shakes his head, and Zach has come to like his stubbornness, the way he sets himself to a task and doesn't budge from it. The way he asks questions, and the thoughtful way he considers their answers. None of which Zach has time to admire now, not with the storm reaching a crescendo outside, a burst of light and noise. With them, an orchestra of pleas.

Zach's hands are shaking despite his efforts to keep them still. That must also rattle Eugenio, because he darts a hand out, fingers a hard circle at Zach's wrist and—

"Don't," Zach gasps out.

Then the world goes dark.

5

———

Zach comes back to himself, no longer at the table, but on the bed. Eugenio is sitting in a chair next to him, his hand splayed on the bedspread near Zach's side as if in comfort—but like he's afraid to physically touch him.

"Here." He helps Zach sit up, offering a glass of tepid water, looking at Zach like Zach might lose consciousness again. "I'm really sorry. I didn't know that would happen."

"It usually doesn't." The digital clock says Zach's only been out for a few minutes, long enough for his mouth to go parched. He drains the glass and starts to get up, though his legs are unsteady, the kitchen sink suddenly miles away.

Eugenio takes the glass from him and comes back a minute later with more water. "You were kind of thrashing around. I don't know what language you were speaking."

"Aramaic, probably."

Eugenio absorbs that, sitting himself back in the chair, watching Zach drink.

The bed isn't, objectively, large, but it feels like an open tundra now. Like whatever is still clawing at the doors and windows can see him. He's wrung out, exposed, scared for the first time in a long while, not that ghosts will burrow into him, but that they'll use him as an avenue to get to Eugenio. Especially as Eugenio brings a hand up from the bedspread to lie next to Zach's own.

"Is this all right?" Eugenio asks. There's an inch of space between them, air humming, purpled from their overlap in auras. Zach should tell him *no*. Should tell him to drive away, back to someplace simpler. Safer.

Eugenio's tattoos undulate, shifting, patterns like the flutter of fabric. Zach's own shirt is sweat-stuck to his back; he reaches to pull it from his skin. "I must have been pretty out of it."

Eugenio nods, leaning forward. His lips are next to Zach's cheek, and it wouldn't take much to turn into his touch. "Zach"—he says his name the way Zach might an incantation —"you scared me."

Said simply, but with enough feeling that Zach leans away from him. Because they shouldn't. Not as the sky rolls with thunder and the rain sheets down. Not with ghosts knocking on the walls.

Zach's skin is clammy, his sweat cooling in the now-chilly cabin. He doesn't trust himself to make it to the little shower stall, doesn't trust that he'll be able to stand once he's there. He wipes a hand across his forehead. Sleeping in his clothes will be gross, but he's slept in worse.

"C'mon." Eugenio offers his hand up. "Can't imagine you're feeling that great."

Zach imagines the collision of their palms, the crackle and static of their auras, how his rubbery legs won't be enough to hold him. "I'm good."

"You'll feel like shit in the morning if you don't at least rinse off," Eugenio says. "Consider it community service, since I'm sleeping here too."

And right, the bed. Though Zach has no idea how they're going to share. Not with the air between them still alight.

He leans on Eugenio's shoulder as they traverse the room. It's not a large space, but it takes them a while to get there, Zach stopping every few steps to catch his breath. When they reach the bathroom, he collapses on the closed toilet seat while Eugenio runs the shower, trying to coax hot water from the recalcitrant water heater.

Zach manages to extract his hearing aid from his ear, tucking it into the case by the sink. His hand is heavy, his movements like swimming through syrup. "I should probably just wash my face. I don't know if I'll be able to make it through a shower."

"I'll help." Eugenio says it with the kind of finality that makes it hard to argue. He tugs off his shirt. Shirtless, Eugenio's aura is brighter, warm like a campfire in the dark. He reaches for Zach's shirt then stops. "We don't have to. I mean. If you just want to rinse off."

Though the prospect of giving himself a wipe down with a lukewarm washcloth is vastly less appealing than a hot shower. Zach takes several clarifying inhales then peels his shirt up, tossing it to the tiled bathroom floor. His skin feels tight, not from dehydration, but like whatever seizure or trance put his bones back too tight. His fingers are numb on the waistband of his pants. He fumbles for a minute, before Eugenio bats him away, hand trailing energy down Zach's stomach, before sliding the button from its hole and easing down his zipper.

"You don't have to," Zach says, when Eugenio goes for his own pants. "If you just want to wait and make sure I don't collapse, I'll probably be all right."

"Easier not to let you fall than to try to scrape you off the floor of the shower. Plus that drain is scarier than anything outside." He smiles like that's just common sense, then unbuckles his belt.

And Zach has seen him mostly naked, in his shorts as he comes out of the bathroom in the morning. He's broad, with a slathering of muscle, solid and reassuring in a way that Zach wants to lean on, especially now, when he can't steady his hands.

It takes some maneuvering to get into the shower, since getting up makes him feel even dizzier. There's enough space for him to turn around, enough space to fall. But not enough space for Eugenio in with him. Unless they're touching.

The shower smells like the soap Eugenio uses, a scent like a cleaner version of the woods. Zach lets the spray warm him for a minute. Eugenio is standing close behind him, and Zach thought about this, a dozen times over the past few days. It's different, wrung out, with a post-spectral hangover. Tiredness coats the back of his tongue. He fumbles for the shampoo, nearly knocking the bottle off the shelf.

Eugenio reaches past him, taking the bottle. He still has that leather bracelet on, though it's getting soaked.

"Don't you want to take that off?" Zach asks.

Eugenio looks down at the cuff like he's surprised it's there. He works the buckle, unclasping it, and tossing the bracelet onto the sink.

Zach was expecting more tattoos. Instead, it's a blank expanse of skin interrupted by a single unmoving design. Something Eugenio hides, tucking his wrist into his hip. Like they're not both almost naked, having kept on their shorts. For deniability that feels as thin as the fabric separating them. "I could wash your hair," Eugenio says. "If you want."

Zach's arms are leaden, the steam only somewhat loosening the muscles of his back. Still, this feels intimate, maybe more than if they kissed. Which Zach's currently too tired to think about doing except in the abstract. He's grateful that his back is to Eugenio, that there's only so much space between him and the wall. He leans forward, ducking down so that Eugenio has better access to his hair. There's the faint sound of shampoo being poured out, then Eugenio's hand at his hip.

"Is this OK?" Eugenio asks.

Like being in a warm shower with Eugenio would somehow be *worse* than getting smacked by ghosts. Despite the steam, his throat feels hoarse. "This is good."

It's been a long time since Zach had anyone wash his hair for him. Possibly a trip to the barber or a perfunctory wash from another hunter when he managed to fracture both wrists taking a hard fall. Eugenio stands close. His chest occasionally brushes Zach's back. He rubs shampoo into Zach's hair, massaging it, fingers against Zach's scalp. Zach lets out an involuntary noise. Possibly a moan.

Eugenio laughs at that, a laugh that vibrates pleasantly against Zach's skin. His hands are strong, especially when he presses his thumbs to the base of Zach's skull, massaging. Something in Zach's spine unwinds. It's nice, almost inarticulably so. Dangerous, possibly. With the long howl of the storm outside bearing the insistence of lost souls. Calling to him to resolve their earthly business—to have some wrong righted or get the answer to a long-forgotten question. When he first took up ghost-hunting, he thought it'd be closer to being a private investigator, that if he dealt with ghosts fairly, they'd do the same with him.

Then one flung him across a room.

Shampoo foam drips down Zach's ears, onto his neck and shoulders. "Here." It takes some doing, but he manages to get under the spray to rinse off. He feels sleepy, but less tired. Warm in a way he hasn't felt like in a long time. Cared for, especially when Eugenio hands him a washcloth.

"I can probably get the rest," Zach says.

"Okay." Though Eugenio doesn't move right away.

And Zach should focus on the tiled wall of the shower, on the feel of his body knitting itself back together, on the blanket of silence now comforting his mind. Cleared of other thoughts, it's hard not to notice that Eugenio is almost naked. Dripping. Water beads his eyelashes and works its way down his chest. His shorts cling.

Zach's aura gives a hopeful pulse. "Thank you. For, uh, washing my hair."

"It's not really a hardship." Eugenio's tattoos are harder to discern in the steam. Patterns form and disperse. Zach wants to put his hands on them. To feel their texture, to see what they might do if he pressed a kiss to Eugenio's belly. What they might do if Zach made him laugh or brought him a cup of coffee in the morning, Eugenio groaning that he didn't want to get up and that ghosts are more active at night anyway. "I should let you finish," Eugenio says, and steps out of the shower before Zach can tell him not to go.

Zach scrubs himself down with soap, enjoying the slight abrasion of the washcloth. The tension steams from his pores. When he gets out, Eugenio is sitting on the closed toilet, probably waiting to make sure Zach didn't fall down. He has a towel wrapped around his waist and another draped on his shoulders. He hands Zach one from a pile of them.

"I should be okay," Zach says, though it feels oddly modest, given they're about to sleep in the same bed.

Eugenio gets up, studying him like he's expecting Zach to dissolve or collapse. "Yell if you need anything."

When Zach gets out of the bathroom a few minutes later, Eugenio's already in bed. He's got his glasses back on. A bottle of water sits on the rickety little nightstand by him. There's one by Zach's as well. Eugenio shuts the book he's reading, marking the page with an actual bookmark. And Zach wants nothing more than to slide under the covers, to twine himself up in Eugenio even if they were strangers to each other a few days ago. To rest his head on Eugenio's collarbone and listen to him as he reads.

Zach settles for making it into his side of the bed. There isn't a TV. The only lights in the room are lamps and the red glow of Eugenio's aura like a dimmed candle. The bed—his side of the bed—is cool, though there's a gradient of heat from where Eugenio is lying.

Zach settles with his still damp hair on the pillow. "Has the storm died down? It's hard to tell without my hearing aid in."

"It has." A hand, one on Zach's shoulder, comforting. "Is this alright?"

Zach should shrug him off. It'd be safer that way, for both of them. He doesn't. Instead, he nods, cheek brushing against the pillow.

"I didn't know if... I don't know how it works," Eugenio says. "If there are certain rules or whatever."

"That makes two of us." Zach yawns. It's warm under the bedclothes, Eugenio like a furnace next to him. "It's sort of like static. I don't know, it's hard to explain. It builds up and then there's a discharge. Maybe they'll leave me alone for a little while."

"That must make it hard." Eugenio brushes his hand into the hair at the nape of Zach's neck. "Being close to people."

Zach swallows slightly around the lump in his throat. "It does. It's been a little while since I've been with anyone." An understatement, because the last guy he dated got rightly scared off when a ghost started tossing things around his kitchen. Zach swept up the shards of glass and deleted all his dating apps.

It was easier not to answer the question of "What do you do?" with "I hunt ghosts. And sometimes they hunt me." It was easier being on his own without worrying there was something a ghost could latch onto. Easier. Uncomplicated. Unlike the slow stroke of Eugenio's hand up his shoulder, and the way he held Zach up when Zach felt like he was going to crumble to dust.

"It's been a little while," Eugenio says, "for me too."

Zach turns at that. Because Eugenio is handsome, in a way that commands attention, from Zach and probably from a hundred spirits swirling above the cabin. His thoughts must show because Eugenio adds, "You look surprised."

"You know, just with—" Zach motions to him. "You don't seem like a person who'd be alone."

A smile, this one pleased. "Neither do you."

"I'm not alone. That's the problem. There's always a ghost around. When I was young, I used to dream about going to Antarctica or to space, just to get away from all of this."

Eugenio's smile deepens. Zach studies the fringe of his eyelashes, the slight pink tinge of his cheeks. He has a scar through one eyebrow, something silvery and almost invisible, the kind with a story behind it. "Could be aliens haunting up there," Eugenio says. "Or penguin spirits."

Zach laughs at that. "Penguins would probably be easier."

"It'd probably be hard to live there. Especially since your feet are already cold."

Zach shifts his legs under the blankets.

"It's OK. I don't mind." Another slow stroke of his hand in Zach's hair. He rubs the end of one curl between his fingers. "Your hair's soft."

"Are you surprised?"

"A little."

Like he thought about it the way Zach thought about the bare skin at his wrist.

"Sorry," Zach says. "For laughing at you earlier. When you got thrown across the room. I guess I got paid back for that, huh?"

"Yeah, I got a pretty nice bruise going on my ass." He pets Zach's hair again. "Everything feels clearer out here. Usually, I can feel a presence in a room, but it's like seeing it through water. Now, it's all sharper. Here, see." Eugenio extends his arm. His tattoos flow in calm sine waves.

"What do you think is causing that?"

"Zach"—his name breathed out, in a tone of slight exasperation—"you honestly don't know?"

Outside, the wind howls, whatever ghosts either blown away in the passing storm or gone to easier haunts. Zach feels around the room for a channel of energy. It only takes a second to find one. A bright vein of it, tangibly clear, with a reddish tinge like magma. He swallows. "Yeah, I guess I see what you mean."

"Do you think you'll be able to sleep?"

Zach nods. If they lie like this any longer, he'll be asleep anyway. "Storm's quieted down. Sometimes right after a big blow up, they can't see me. Makes it a little easier."

Eugenio's hand combs back through his hair. "Sleep," he says, and so Zach does.

When Zach wakes up, it's almost morning, gray light coming in the windows. Eugenio's curled with his chest to Zach's back, arm thrown across him. It's warm, pleasant, waking like coming ashore from a warm pool to a sunny beach. He shifts to get the bottle of water from the puddle it sweated onto the nightstand. Eugenio grunts an objection, face in the short hairs of Zach's neck, body solid behind him, like a barrier between Zach and the rest of the world.

Eugenio's aura quieted in sleep. It clings to him like the pale light of dawn, tinged purplish where it overlaps with Zach's. His wrist is at Zach's waist, held against his skin. Warm from his pulse and from something else there too, whatever tattoo there aglow, light spilling from it.

"Hey," Zach says, trying to move himself again. Another objection, a grunt. Lips at the back of his neck, soft. Zach's body aches from being spiritually run over. From the sensation of it, the slight rub of Eugenio's nose and the press of his mouth and how, eventually, they'll have to get up and do things—like summon ghosts—and how much Zach doesn't want to.

"Can we stay here?" Zach says.

Eugenio laughs at that. "You tell me."

They're probably a beacon in the half-morning light for whatever restless spirits are still swirling around. Because of course they'll find him. Both of them. Curled up like this together. A bridge, a spiritual red carpet, a vulnerability, all weighed against the feel of Eugenio against him and the possibility that, if they worked hard enough, maybe things could turn out okay.

"You should know," Zach says, "ghosts latch onto connections between people. It's like an entryway into the person."

He expects Eugenio to roll away, to put his feet on the inevitably chilly floorboards, and the safety of space between them. He tightens his arms instead. "I know."

Which is enough to make Zach turn in surprise.

"You think I didn't do the reading?" Eugenio has that smile again, teasing, with his eyes crinkling at the edges. "How else am I gonna make ghost hunter honor roll?"

"I thought you wouldn't... It could be dangerous."

Eugenio raises an eyebrow at that. "What could be?"

Like it's not obvious in the contact of their bodies, or the way he'd held Zach up in the shower. Or the way Zach's been looking at him. Thinking about him. "If we were together."

Eugenio casts a look between them. "They might come in and break some dishes?"

"Not exactly. Ghosts like people who can see them. Sense them. Otherwise they wouldn't have put on that show last night. Things can get bad."

"Has that happened to you before?"

"A possession? To me, once. But to other people? Not yet. But I've never been with someone who thought any of this stuff was real."

"Okay."

"Okay?"

A shrug, a fond expression, Eugenio's eyes unlensed by glasses. "So *if* they decide that we're targets and *if* we somehow can't protect against them, then we'll tell them to fuck off." Said with a confident roll of his shoulders, a shivering of his tattoos.

Brash enough that Zach kisses him, an awkward kiss,

given the angle, their mouths still fuzzed with sleep. A kiss Eugenio leans into, ushering Zach down, until they're slotted together.

A kiss that goes on for a while, Zach's aura glowing brighter, and the answering shine of Eugenio's, as the light transitions into dawn, then full daylight.

Eventually they pull apart. Zach's mouth stings pleasantly from Eugenio's morning stubble. There are red marks on Eugenio's neck. Zach rubs his thumb over one.

"You trying to warn away malicious spirits through hickeys?" Eugenio asks.

Zach flushes at that. "No."

Eugenio kisses him again. "You getting up? I could use some coffee."

"You're not gonna come and take over halfway through when I'm not doing it right?" The way he did the day before, which feels like far more than twenty-four hours ago.

Another kiss. "I might."

Zach doesn't want to leave this bed or this cabin or the sheltering circle of energy around them. Even if he needs caffeine, another hot shower, to brush his teeth and find out what it's like to kiss Eugenio in the kitchen, on the creaking couch. Hell, across the surface of a scrying table, and let ghosts try to take them. He pulls back. "Let me go make you some coffee."

And Eugenio rewards him with another smile.

The day passes easily. The ghosts have tired themselves out, apparently, or are regrouping, lurking like spiritual mist on the horizon. They drink coffee out on the porch, Eugenio grumbling at the cold until Zach loans him a sweatshirt that's too small across the shoulders and too long in the arms.

Eugenio cooks breakfast, tattoos flickering contentedly,

serving Zach a plate heaped with eggs with tomatoes and onions, and thick corn pancakes folded around a salty white cheese.

"It's been a while since I ate like this," Zach says around a mouthful.

"It's just eggs. Besides, you can't cook?"

"Enough to keep me going."

"That's not really a way to live."

"It's worked thus far."

Eugenio raises his eyebrows as if questioning that but doesn't say anything other than offering Zach more food.

When they're done, Zach clears the table, washing dishes and setting them into the rubber-matted drying rack.

"I was thinking," Eugenio says, "we might try something else for scrying."

"What kind of thing?" Because Zach doesn't want to spend another day fruitlessly searching for local spirits, especially when Eugenio kissed him as his wrists were plunged into soapy water, then slid next to him to dry dishes.

"Ghosts are attracted to connections between people. So maybe, instead of waiting for one to show up, we should lure it here."

Zach blinks at that, trying to process the chain of logic. "I don't think that's gonna work for general ghost-hunting purposes." And he goes red at the idea of mentioning that to D'Spara as what solidified Eugenio's ability to scry.

"I didn't mean it like that." Eugenio's mouth twitches in amusement. "Does the connection have to be physical?"

Zach shakes his head. "Ghosts see us, but mostly auras. Where they overlap or how they're shifting. Like when you were playing with those lots, I could feel it."

"Oh, you could?" Eugenio says mock innocently.

"Yeah, look where that got us."

Eugenio slides two fingers under his own shirt collar, against the marks that have come up purple. "Could be worse. But let's try something a little different."

They end up at the scrying table, Eugenio holding a mug of late-morning coffee, Zach's stomach tight with nerves. It's a cool, damp day, mist rising from the forest outside, visible through the translucent curtains draping the windows. Ghost weather.

"How'd you want to do this?" Zach asks.

Eugenio waves a hand over the table as if expecting its sigils to glow. It remains wood and hinges. "Just, if they're looking for a connection, let's give them one."

Which doesn't really answer Zach's question. "Like an entry point?"

"More like a date."

Zach doesn't point out that it's eleven in the morning. That they've been in each other's company for the past three days. That he can't remember the last date he went on that wasn't ascertaining that someone looked like their photo on a hookup app. "Um, okay."

Eugenio's smile broadens. "Why do you look like you'd rather face down a ghost?"

"I understand them better, I guess," Zach blurts, too honest, except for Eugenio's hand over his in reassurance.

"So, Zach," Eugenio says, like they're meeting for the first time, like they're out at a bar and not in a cabin in the middle of nowhere, "what do you like to do for fun?"

"Really?" Zach asks incredulously.

"Not going to answer the question?"

"I assumed you'd have a little more game than that, given—" He gestures to Eugenio.

Eugenio laughs at that. "You think I'm just coasting on

my good looks?" He raises his eyebrows, including the one bisected by a scar, and Zach wants to know about that, and what Eugenio likes to do for fun that's not spending a week in a cabin with someone who can, but doesn't want to, hear ghosts.

All of which is too much to say, so Zach manages, "Mostly I hunt ghosts. For fun, I mean."

"Just that?"

"I read about hunting ghosts too." Because there's always research and preparation work and an endless stream of information D'Spara gives that's up to Zach to make sense of.

"How about this—for vacation, beach or mountains?"

"Beach. Definitely beach."

"Really?"

"Harder to hear ghosts with the ocean. And I like swimming."

"Maybe we should go some time."

And Zach gets a visual of Eugenio there, shirtless, smeared with sunscreen, laughing. Someplace where the surf and shore birds could drown out everything else. "How about you?"

"Both, I guess. Though I'm told I can be a little pushy when it comes to vacation scheduling."

"Doesn't sound like you," Zach says, and Eugenio knocks his shoulder against his. "Is it my turn to ask something?"

"Sure, if you want it to be."

Zach considers all of the this or that questions: Coffee or tea, which he knows. Mornings or evenings, which he also knows. A dozen other possibilities, all of which seem facile, inauthentic to establish whatever they need to do to lure a ghost to them. "Where'd you learn how to cook like that?"

Eugenio smiles. "My parents worked all the time when I

was growing up. Professors"—with a *What can you do?* shrug —"so I taught myself. I didn't really know how to make Venezuelan food. That's where they're from. It was sort of figuring that part of myself out too."

"My mom would like that. I mean, she cooks a lot. I think she's disappointed because the only thing any of us knows how to make is takeout or a mess. The first time I tried to cook bacon, I think I nearly burned my apartment down. I'd never seen it made before 'cause they keep kosher."

"I could teach you."

Zach doesn't say that he looked up a bunch of YouTube videos that told him to just stick bacon on a sheet tray in the oven, instead imagining Eugenio in one of the cramped kitchens of Zach's temporary apartments frowning over Zach's hand-me-down cookware and fussing at him to eat more. It's not a bad picture. "That'd be, uh, all right. If you wanted."

With that, Eugenio's smile. "Ask me something else."

"When you went back to the Walmart, what'd you get?" Zach expects something boring, like socks or maybe an ingredient Zach doesn't know how to cook with.

Instead Eugenio looks faintly embarrassed. Or not embarrassed, just a pleased kind of flush. "Dessert stuff. Nondairy. I've never made it before, but the recipe looks doable." Like he bought stuff specifically to cook *for* Zach.

From there, it is like a date, though one in which they both look at the carved surface of the table periodically, watching for telltale signs of another entity. Eventually, though, they migrate from table to porch, porch to couch, couch to kitchen as Eugenio cooks and explains what he's cooking, and Zach tries to listen attentively while also palming his back and hips.

They end up in bed, still talking, making out lazily while afternoon shifts into twilight. Eugenio's shirt ends up tossed somewhere. Zach spends a while mouthing at his tattoos, some of which extend to his waistband. And true to his assertion, he has a nice bruise going on his ass, one he laughs when Zach mentions, a laugh that turns breathier as they kiss, as they rock together, the world for once kept outside the creaking cabin walls.

Afterward, Zach drifts for a while, Eugenio's hand in his hair, Eugenio reading a book about ghost-hunting that Zach teases him for, though he's read it too.

When Zach wakes up, it's almost night and there's a ghost standing at the foot of the bed.

It must have died in the nearby river because it looks half drowned, long dark hair like seaweed and a smudge for a mouth. Before he saw his first ghost, he expected them to all be pale, papery things. This one is as smooth as polished stone, white as the belly of a fish. Also, it's screaming.

There's no sound, just the image of terror, a rictus for a mouth, like whatever dark tumble it took into the water has been going on since it fell.

And *fuck*, he didn't think to put his bag of lots on the bedside table, or his cards, or anything that would help banish it. He stirs, enough to wake Eugenio, who's asleep beside him, book abandoned. He startles awake with a bitten-off objection before going, "Oh. Oh shit."

"You can see them?"

Eugenio goes pale, then nods. "What should we do?"

Run. But, of course, they can't, and fuck, he shouldn't have... they shouldn't have... Even if Zach felt lighter than he had in weeks. Months. Possibly longer. "Where's that knife?" Zach says.

Eugenio fumbles in the bedtable drawer, tossing things

out of it, until he brings up a knife. Zach expected something old, leather clad, symbols burned in the sheath. This looks closer to a large pocketknife, with multitools set into one handle. Too new, too shiny for interrogating a ghost.

The figure's still screaming, though it's shifted somehow, as if silence could be quieter. As if seeing them for the first time. It gets a look Zach would almost call quizzical, if not for the tangle of hair in its face.

"What do you want?" Zach says finally.

Eugenio glances at him, and Zach shrugs.

The ghost gives another wordless cry, one that embeds in Zach's brain like a headache. With it, a wave of diffuse nausea.

Next to him, Eugenio gasps a breath.

"Are you OK?"

A headshake, and when he opens his mouth, river water comes out. A splash of it, over the edge of the bed, on the floorboards, and fuck, the ghost isn't just drowned, it's taking Eugenio with it.

Zach scrambles for the knife, popping the blade out, then stabbing uselessly at the air where the ghost is. He meets no resistance. The scraps of the figure scatter then reassemble. Eugenio heaves another mouthful of water.

"Fuck off," Zach tries. The ghost makes a face like it's laughing. More water, a larger volume this time. And the walls are crying now, the floorboards coughing up a film like silt. It's possible they'll both be drowned. That he spent a last perfect day among the living only to be pulled under.

The lightning storm of pain in his head intensifies, making it hard to remember anything he's learned, not with Eugenio next to him expelling more water. His skin has gone pale, bluish, like he can't pull enough air, and Zach can't think, doesn't think, just grabs onto Eugenio's wrist, encased in its leather cuff. His hand is frantic at the buckle, discarding it, finding the skin there inscribed with a tattoo. An unmoving one. Two letters, ones familiar from Zach's lots. A kaf and a lamed. Yes and no, simultaneously.

He presses his thumb between them, trying to force some of his aura into Eugenio, like that will get oxygen to his lungs.

A noise. A sound like paper tearing, and the ghost flickers. Zach does it again, willing his energy outward. To provide a bridge, a distraction, an invitation. A spiritual *leave him the fuck alone.*

And the ghost almost laughs as it turns its attentions from Eugenio to him.

There's a crash, like the clap of an overhead thunderstorm. A downpour of rain. The floorboards are blackened now, water gushing up around them, higher, higher. Zach presses his hand against the letters again. "Whatever you are, you're not that anymore."

The ghost looks at him, head slightly tilted.

"I don't know what's after this," Zach says. "Maybe it's heaven. Or a long endless tunnel. Maybe it's nothing, just sleep."

Thunder rumbles its disapproval. The floors put forth more water. Eugenio goes blue at his lips, eyes bulging, desperate.

"I don't think of death as any of those things," Zach says. "Just a mountain I can't see the other side of." He tightens a hand at Eugenio's wrist, watching the blur of their auras. "There's nothing here for you. If you stay here, there'll be nothing left of you."

Eugenio goes limp next to him.

"Fuck. Fuck, fuck, fuck." Zach pushes him over onto his side, a long pour of water on the floor, a hand on his back, between his shoulder blades. Even his tattoos have slowed under his skin. His eyes are white, clouded, and then he speaks with someone else's voice, a croaked *What if*—without resolution.

What if— A question. *The* question, like standing with your toes at the edge of a crumbling cliff's edge, afraid to fall into the dark canyon below. *What if*—

"I don't know," Zach says. "I'm not meant to know. But I can tell you that whatever's next can't be worse than being wrapped up forever in fear."

Eugenio's eyes go a brief incandescent white like an old lightbulb blinking out.

Then the ghost is gone, the room cleared of its mud and silt, its floors bone dry. None of which matters because Eugenio isn't moving. Isn't breathing.

Zach taps him, hand against his face, like Eugenio is merely sleeping. Nothing. His hand falls limply across the bedspread. His shirtfront is wet with river water. His tattoos have stilled, and that might be the worst of it, the possibility that Eugenio is really gone.

Panic overtakes Zach, heart drumbeating against his constricted chest. He shakes Eugenio again, then fumbles for his hand. Two fingers against his inscribed wrist. A pulse, diminished but present. The kaf and lamed glow faintly.

Zach pulls them to his lips, kissing them, tendrils of his aura projecting out like an energetic causeway between them, bright enough that it's almost tangible. Power drains from him, a decreasing battery, a toll.

Eugenio doesn't stir, though his tattoos glow more fiercely. Darkness starts to impinge on Zach's vision. He presses on. Another pulse of energy jumps between them. It cascades around Eugenio's body, a shower of sparks, a match touched to a fuse, until it amplifies, converges, becomes almost a breathing thing, the connection between them a great loop of light.

Eugenio coughs awake, blinking back into consciousness. His tattoos start slow circuits around his arms. "You miss me?" he says, with a smile, and Zach kisses him, deeply, encompassingly, a *yes* that Eugenio laughs into.

Eugenio pulls back after a minute. "My mouth tastes like I swallowed most of the Susquehanna."

"Maybe don't get up for a second." Because Zach's emptied, weightless, exhausted. His hand finds Eugenio's wrist, grasping it. They lie like that for a few minutes, Zach grateful for the sound of Eugenio's breath.

Eugenio shifts his wrist in Zach's hold, sitting up halfway and examining the ink there. "Oh."

"You could have said you knew what those letters were," Zach says, "since you got them there and all."

"I didn't. That's a fate tattoo. It takes whatever shape it needs to. Usually, it fades pretty quickly."

Zach studies the design. Two letters—kaf and lamed. *Yes* and *no*. The lamed is blurred at the edges, like it's going out of focus, dissolving back into skin around it. The kaf remains, unambiguous. *Yes.* "What'd you ask the lots?"

Eugenio smiles. "If I'd make it through this." He adjusts his wrist in Zach's grip, tapping on the letter that shows no sign of fading. "If we'd be together."

And Zach brings the tattoo to his mouth, lips at the highway of veins. Eugenio makes a contented noise, until Zach kisses him there, on the outcropping of his wrist bones and in the cup of his palm, and at the callused tip of each finger, drawing an exhale, a pleased incantation of Zach's name.

When he pulls back, his eyes are wet, possibly from

residual river water, though perhaps not with the look Eugenio's giving him, with the stability of his palm against Zach's face.

"Thank you," Eugenio says. "For bringing me back."

"You should probably know—there might be side effects. Of the possession. After I got back, I could sense things I couldn't before. The ghosts got worse or my vision got better."

Eugenio shuts his eyes like he's doing a self-assessment. Zach watches the line of his eyelashes against his cheek, wondering what life will be like, outside this bed, outside this cabin. If he'll be able to look at Eugenio and not see his eyes glassed over, thrashing, desperate. If Eugenio will always have some part of himself in another world. If he'll thank Zach for that or blame him.

There's a light between them, the after-effects of the bridge. Eugenio opens his eyes, bringing up his palm. In the valley of it, he's holding a little dose of light. One that's glowing a faint but unmistakable purple.

"I think things might be a little different after this," he says, and Zach kisses him again, river water and all.

THREE DAYS LATER, THEY PULL IN AT A REST STOP ON ROUTE 95. The parking lot is a sea of older sedans and working vehicles. Families stretch and squabble. Inside, the rest stop smells like cinnamon buns and floor cleaner, chasing the odor of the woods from Zach's nose.

Eugenio passed out about fifteen minutes into their drive, head pillowed on Zach's rolled up jacket, hands aglow with purple light, hair slightly mussed from the action of Zach's fingers.

That light intensified over their days together, a trace of it at Eugenio's hands, down his back, in the hollows of his knees. Places Zach explored, slowly, achingly, after waking up with no long call of spirits, with no demanding figures at the foot of his bed. Just quiet and Eugenio, the light between them growing stronger.

Now it feels obvious, a connection between them like a neon sign, even in the harsh almost-surgical lighting of the rest stop.

"What do you want to eat?" Zach asks.

Eugenio studies the food court skeptically, before rattling off an order complicated enough that Zach says, "Text that to me."

Eugenio does, then kisses Zach on his cheek, an unthinking little kiss that makes Zach glow like the basin of Eugenio's palms.

Eugenio glances around. "I don't see anything." Because he woke up the day after his possession, complaining that ghosts were fogging his vision like smudged glasses. Sight that clarified with the application of coffee, and Zach's hand in his as they explored the woods around the cabin, its hollows still brimming with ghosts.

It was easy, the two of them together, to say, "What troubles you friend?" To listen to ghosts' pleas and fears. To send them gently into the world beyond with a careful flick of Eugenio's wrist, his fingers still entwined with Zach's.

Here the food court is flooded with light, the only cries that of irate toddlers. Zach listens for that familiar river of energy, for the current that sweeps over the world, carrying with it the complaints of the dead. "Maybe they're not here."

"Then we'll just have to keep driving," Eugenio says.

"Yeah." Zach smiles at that. "Yeah, I guess we will."

ORDINARY GHOSTS

1

———

ALEX ISN'T ONE OF THOSE LIBRARIANS WHO SHUSHES PEOPLE—libraries are community spaces and communities don't come from librarians constantly pressing their fingers to pursed lips. Still, it's hard not to tap the *Please be courteous to other patrons* sign when the man comes bounding up.

Some people have noisy auras.

Not that Alex believes in auras, specifically. Not the way Sofia does. He doesn't *not* believe in auras either, especially when this particular patron rattles up and immediately chucks a half a dozen books on the checkout desk. The guy is tall—six four or six five, the demarcation above which men on dating apps stop lying about their height. Alex is five nine. He lists his height at five nine.

Unlike Alex, the man on the other side of the desk is long and lean. Gangly if Alex isn't being charitable. *Handsome for a nuisance* if he is.

He hasn't done anything nuisance-y quite yet, but Alex has a sense for patron attitudes he refuses to call a sixth sense. He can tell if someone is going to be annoying using his other five senses, thanks. So he puts on his approximation of a customer service face: less of a scowl, but the implication of one is still there.

The guy smiles as if on reflex—as if someone early in his life told him that his smile was his most persuasive feature. *Smile* is underselling it. This is a grin, bright, unassuming, unthreatening...but with a flash of teeth that says he wants something.

Alex makes a noise that is in no way a grunt. In the order of things Alex likes about librarian-ing, working with young people is the first. Books are a close second. Occasionally getting to throw library events with punk concerts is a third.

Library adults who want something more complicated than fines resolved are pretty near the bottom of the list. Hopefully this guy, who's about to check out—Alex glances at the stack—most of the library's books about the occult just wants to know where the restroom is. Alex spends a lot of his day directing people to the restroom.

It's also possible he's one of those busybody fucks who objects to the public library having books for the *public* and wants these books removed from these shelves lest they prove a bad influence on the youth. Alex prides himself on being...not a bad influence, but at least the adult who the scowly kids with dyed black hair and too many piercings can talk to. Some things are intergenerational.

Alex squares his shoulders and prepares himself for the politest version of a fight.

The man's smile doesn't harden, exactly, but something in it goes *stubborn* as if he isn't leaving here with less than a yes. "I heard you have ghost-hunting equipment I can rent. Check out. Borrow."

"I—" Alex's begins. "What?"

"Here." The man digs something from a folder and hands it to Alex. Whatever Alex expected, it wasn't what this turns out to be—a print-out of the library's materials lending list. Three items are circled: an EMF meter; EVP recorder; flashlight.

Alex should be happy someone is using the materials-library inventory. It makes it easier to justify in the budget. When Alex went to library school, he didn't realize exactly how much of his life he'd spend justifying things in the budget to people who consider libraries one step away from communism. Alex considers the library exactly zero steps away from communism, but he's developed the sense not to say that in budget meetings.

Alex should say something productive like *How'd you hear about the materials library?* since most of the people who know about it are adults who come in with their kids and go "shopping" for toys. For them, Alex pretends to ring up at the library counter and makes fake cash register noises to get the kids to giggle. Growing up with used toys that have to go back after three weeks is rough; he hopes making silly bell and cha-ching noises helps a little.

Instead, Alex says, "Did you print our inventory list?" and doesn't bite back the skepticism in his voice.

For whatever reason, the man's grin goes pleased. The same noisiness is there like an atmosphere around him, a faint shush like the applause of a crowd. *He's gonna be a problem,* Alex thinks. And Alex is absolutely and one hundred percent not psychic—there's no such thing as real auras or ghosts or premonitions—so this is just intuition. A *hunch.*

"Helps to be prepared," the man says. He proffers his library card like he's proving he's qualified to patronize this particular branch. *Jake Fischer* is written on the name slot in neat print. He glances at Alex examining it as if he expects Alex to react.

Alex amends his previous assessment of *nuisance* to *well-*

organized nuisance, objectively the most dangerous kind. Still there's no reason he can't lend out a meter that produces random beeps if this guy—*Jake*—wants to spend his night screwing around with it.

"Yeah, c'mon." Alex waves Jake on.

Something about that makes Jake laugh. His laugh isn't loud, exactly, but it echoes off the shelves, and when he's done, he turns to Alex expectantly.

"Shush," Alex says, on reflex, and that gets Jake going again.

Alex won't dwell, not on Jake and Jake's laugh. "C'mon," he says, again, and doesn't wait to see if Jake follows.

Even within the library stacks, the materials lending area is especially quiet. It's housed in a long narrow room with doors on each end that Alex keeps propped open to allow for ventilation and so that people don't go in there to fuck or get high. Materials sit on various shelves: board games, crafting supplies, power tools.

It's probably just the effect of being a late afternoon in Rhode Island in October, but a shadow casts over the room, one that wasn't there before. Alex turns to find Jake hovering at his back. Alex hopes he isn't going to be mugged. They have security cameras, but Alex doesn't like dealing with cops.

Jake, perhaps sensing his unease, smiles that same grin of his. "Wow, you have a lot of stuff in here!" He picks something up—one of the kids' games—shakes it, then replaces it on the shelf, looking contrite. "Oops, sorry."

"They're toys," Alex says, unnecessarily. "They're meant to be played with."

Jake laughs again, a laugh that heaves his shoulders, which aren't as narrow as Alex first clocked. "I guess that's what I'm doing, right? Only with grown-up toys?"

He asks it like he expects Alex to respond. Alex's official position on what anyone borrows from the library is *neutral.* Libraries are for communities and Alex is here to serve the *community.* Even if Jake wants equipment that doesn't actually do anything.

"Toys are supposed to be fun," Alex shoots back. He clicks his mouth shut a second too late. He should have just shut up. He doesn't want to deal with a patron *complaint.* Because that means paperwork, the kind he used to like when he started librarian-ing but he now thinks of as *pain in the ass*-work.

Jake gives him another of those looks, an assessment of reddish-brown eyelashes. Alex is not looking at his eyes, which are greenish gray and curious, or his eyelashes, which are long like the rest of him, or his hands that look more work-roughened than Alex would have expected from a guy wearing a cardigan.

Maybe Alex shouldn't judge. He also sometimes wears cardigans, though his tend to have a bunch of safety pins in them and paint spatters from his cousin's studio.

"Depends on your definition of fun," Jake says eventually.

"Sure." Alex says it less to agree and more to get out this conversation. What he should be doing is hauling the ghost-hunting equipment out, scanning Jake's library card, and hoping that someone else is working when Jake returns them inevitably covered in mud or fake ectoplasm or whatever. What he is doing is standing here waiting for Jake to respond as if he's encouraging him.

Especially when Jake smiles. His teeth are especially bright in the half dark. "Do you not believe in ghosts or ghost-hunting?"

"What," Alex replies, and Jake looks like he's about to

repeat himself, as if Alex simply didn't hear him. "Wouldn't not believing in ghosts mean not believing in ghost-hunting?"

That gets another grin. It must be the dim lights of the storage area, but this one is *dazzling*. "Some people believe in ghosts but not that we can catch them." Jake shrugs like he doesn't really understand that but wants to acknowledge it as a valid position just in case.

"You think we can catch ghosts?" And Alex can't help it. He does wiggly fingers to accompany it, the same ones he makes during kids' story time and used to make when his cousin was growing up and he told her tall tales in the dark, a flashlight held under his chin to up the spookiness.

That elicits another shrug. Jake tugs his sweater back over his wrists like he's trying to hide his size beneath lumpy green knit. He grins like he wants to goad Alex into a reaction. Maybe whatever Alex's face is doing—his eyebrows pinch, his mouth defaults to a scowl—constitutes a reaction. "Maybe ghosts don't exist," Jake says. "But some things are worth chasing after, you know?"

Alex's instincts aren't usually wrong. Fast judgments keep you safe. Whoever this Jake guy is, Alex is pretty sure he's *pretending* to be harmless. Alex's internal alarms—ones he refuses to call anything other than instincts—start blaring.

I need to get out of here. Out from a relatively enclosed space with a man who he can't stop looking at. So Alex scans the room until he spots the box of ghost-hunting equipment sitting on the bottom rung of the shelves. A box he doesn't recall seeing before, even if he's been in this part of the library a million times: but there it is, his handwriting on the label of a large bin that's dusted in a layer of chalk-white grit.

Alex grabs the box. "For larger equipment like this, we need to go through the inventory together, just to be sure it comes back in the same condition." A policy Alex instituted the first time someone brought back a busted drill and claimed that Alex had lent it to him that way.

Jake's eyebrows rise. A smile plays around the edges of his lips. "So you assume I'll make it back?"

Alex's official position is that he cares for all of his patrons equally—neutrally. He cares that Jake makes it back exactly as much as he would any other patron. Even as Jake's smile flickers toward uncertainty as if his return is in fact an open question and not a guarantee.

"We'll go through this at the service desk," Alex says, pretending he didn't hear him. Still, as he hauls the ghost-hunting kit through the library, he trades one worry—that Jake is doing something stupid that's a waste of time—for another: that he might be doing something stupid that's also dangerous.

Back in the full light of the service desk, Alex uncaps the box and displays its three pieces of promised equipment.

Jake gestures to something that looks like a small black radio. "May I?" he asks, with the kind of grammatical correctness like he had a childhood of being asked, *I don't know, can you?* as opposed to Alex, who mostly heard *Try it and see.*

Alex should probably tell him *no*, just so he won't be blamed if Jake breaks it. But really who could tell if a *makes shit up* meter is broken or not? So he reaches into the bin... just as Jake does the same.

Jake snatches his hand back like he doesn't want to make even slight but accidental contact with Alex. "Sorry," Jake says, belatedly.

Alex grinds his teeth together *neutrally*. Because he has

no fewer than three earrings in each ear, including his tunnel spacers. He's also got a large rainbow pin stuck to his work lanyard that's holding his ID badge in a holder reading *Fun Isn't Hard If You've Got A Library Card*. If Jake objects to that pin, Alex hopes he does find a ghost—maybe one of a hostile queer elder.

"Sorry," Jake says again, like he's apologizing for apologizing. He stuffs his fingers in his pockets for good measure. His knuckles are faintly bruised, like he's been in a fight and the other guy lost. Alex's *instincts* issue a very clear directive: *This guy is a threat. Get back.*

He's not going to let himself be cowed. Not by some guy in a cardigan, no matter what his eyelashes look like.

So Alex pulls the black radio thing from the box and examines it for some indication of what it's supposed to do. *How do you even catch a ghost?* he doesn't ask. Mostly so Jake doesn't answer.

It's not like Alex is totally unfamiliar with spooky stuff as a concept, even if Sofia's version of psychic powers extends to reading tarot for the neighbors. Her practice is about seasonality and intention and only occasionally selling back gossip at a markup to clients who know what they're paying for, anyway.

A helpful piece of electrical tape—in his own handwriting—tells Alex he's holding an EMF meter. Why he used budget for this, he doesn't remember. There isn't an obvious *on* button. Maybe it's one of those ghost-hunting things that works on vibes.

Except Jake slips his hand between where Alex is holding the meter—the sleeve of his cardigan wrapped carefully around his hand as if he's worried about Alex's gay cooties rubbing off on him—and flips a switch. Instantly, the meter burbles to life, emitting a distinct chattering noise like the one Alex has been vaguely hearing ever since Jake walked in.

Which is…odd. Alex's *hunches* don't usually extend to aural premonitions.

"Looks like it works," Jake says.

"Is this it working?" Alex can't keep his skepticism out of his voice.

Jake laughs, big and delighted. "Yep, that's pretty much what it's supposed to do."

"What does it do if there's a ghost?" Alex asks.

"Who says there isn't one now?" Jake wiggles his fingers like he's specifically doing an impression of Alex from before. "And it does that, but also screams."

"Screams?" Alex repeats.

"Usually, when there's a ghost, most people want to get as far from it as possible."

"Why go through all of this if you're just gonna run away?"

Jake flashes him a grin. "Who says I'm most people?" He quiets the EMF reader, then flicks the flashlight on and off. Finally, he pulls the other piece of equipment that looks like an old candy bar cell phone and taps a button on it. Nothing happens. No hum, no light.

"Guess that's busted," Alex says.

Jake shakes his head. "It's a recorder. When it captures subsonic noise, it transposes the sound into human hearing ranges."

You mean it makes shit up. Neutral. Alex is *neutral*. It's his library's equipment. He bought it even if he can't remember doing so or why. He doesn't care if Jake uses it to find ghosts or as a community-purchased paperweight. He doesn't care how Jake's gaze keeps finding his or the way his eyes shift between gray and green. "Right," Alex says. "Of course."

Jake snorts at that, like Alex told a joke. "Well, it's working. I guess I should get out of your hair." Even if his palm curls, and Alex gets a flick of an image—Jake's hand cradling the back of Alex's head, fingers combing through the shorn spikes of his hair.

Not exactly the usual hunches he gets at the library. But then his instincts have no idea what to make of any of this, so he loads the EMF and EVP and flashlight back into the bin then checks out all the books Jake brought to the desk. "These are due back in three weeks," Alex says.

"That long? I figured I'd have less time for the—" Jake nods toward the bin.

"It's not exactly in high demand. I think you're the first person who's ever checked it out."

If Alex didn't know better, he'd think something in Jake's smile goes a little sad. "Right, gotcha," Jake says. "Well, I should get going, I guess."

Be safe. A thought Alex pushes down. Even if he has a flashed vision of Jake limping back to an apartment to pour betadine on a wound. There's a difference between hunches and worries and Alex is neutral about whatever goes on outside his library doors. Even if something about Jake says he'd try to suture his own wounds. Instead he says, "Good luck."

"Here's hoping." Jake shoulders his bag of books and pulls the box from the counter. "See you around, Angelides."

And it's not until he's been gone for five minutes that Alex realizes he never told Jake his name.

2

A week passes. Alex goes to work, organizes several story time events, designs a seasonal table display for Halloween books. Usually he puts occult books on there just to save himself from having to dig them out when a group of teenage patrons is inevitably *very serious about becoming real witches* for exactly one week. Now, he mostly adds witchy romcoms to the table.

Arranging the table gives him a clear view of the parking lot. If he spends longer than he needs to watching to see if Jake will appear, who'd know? His heart jumps every time a truck pulls in. Not that he's certain Jake drives a truck, but something about him said *truck*.

Jake's truck doesn't appear. Jake doesn't appear. Maybe he's taken the library's occult books and ghost-hunting equipment and...ghosted. Maybe he's stashed them in storage to gather dust the same way Alex did years ago.

That initial acquisition still bothers him. Alex doesn't fear the local city council, but he also doesn't want to have headlines that say *Local Librarian Wastes Taxpayer Money on Ghosts*. The materials library records have always been kind of spotty. Stuff comes, stuff goes, Alex does his best to maintain an inventory that only he really cares about. He's not even sure what year that equipment got bought.

But he's a librarian. Combing through various records in the name of inventory management seems like a great use of his time, and definitely not a way to deflect thinking about Jake and Jake's shoulders and the sharpness in Jake's smile.

So Alex scrolls through old invoices to see when he could have purchased the equipment. It bothers him, a tickle—an itch. The more he looks, the more it bugs him. Until he finds a thin pink sheet stuck in a folder with a note written in his handwriting. *Ghost-hunting equipment—personal donation, Alex Angelides.* Dated almost ten years ago.

What the fuck? Maybe one of Sofia's friends foisted it on him, a gift that annoyed Alex enough that he stuck the kit in a bin and forgot about it for a decade. But no, Alex has a great memory, especially for the things that piss him off. This is a strange blank, like someone took a pencil eraser to his memory.

He's in the process of returning the slip to its folder, the folder to its file hanger, the file hanger to the alphabetized cabinet drawer, when that noise returns. That *hum*, like a frequency in his fillings. *Jake.* Sure enough, Jake's coming through the library doors, but unlike last time, he's not exactly bounding. Fuck, he's limping, a backpack groaning with books pressing on one shoulder. He shuffles past Alex without even an acknowledgment—though the volume of the humming in Alex's back teeth spikes—but he sets up at a table in Alex's direct eyeline. Smiles at the scarred surface of it like he knows he's being watched.

Alex will not be goaded. He does enough goading himself to know when someone's really good at it. Jake takes out book after book after book, arranges them in neat rows based on an organization system Alex can't make out from here. Not that he cares to know. Not that he's leaning over the desk to *snoop*.

Jake rolls his shoulders a few times as if he's preparing for a hard day of studying. Glances over his shoulder exactly once, a look so fleeting Alex almost misses it, like he's daring Alex to watch him read. Like he *wants* Alex to watch him read.

Alex keeps his literal distance. He has other patrons to check on, other shelves to organize, other things to plan. People really think librarians get to read all day, but most of Alex's reading comes at night, when he's holed up in his room at Sofia's house in a bed that used to feel expansive but now just feels empty.

At the end of the day, Jake gathers his things up—books back into his bag, highlighter pens tucked away. He walks past Alex, closer to the desk than is entirely casual, and Alex is preparing himself to say something—even if it's only a growled *Did the library experience meet your expectations?*— when Jake waves a goodbye. And he's already out the door by the time Alex registers that the knuckles on Jake's left hand are once again bruised.

When Alex arrives at the library the following morning, Jake is waiting at the library entrance, holding a steaming cup of coffee. He raises it to Alex in a salute like they're coworkers. Only one other vehicle is sitting in the library parking lot—an older, well-cared-for truck. Alex effing knew it.

"We don't open for another half an hour," Alex says by way of greeting.

Jake pushes his lip out in an exaggerated pout. "I guess I'll wait here."

Alex expected an argument. Wanted one, possibly, a want he's not going examine the way he's not examining the curve of Jake's lower lip. "You can come in if you're quiet."

Jake presses a finger to his mouth like an imitation of a kid trying to keep quiet, then holds the door while Alex wheels in today's cart of craft supplies.

This early, the library is quiet. Or would be if the noise coming off Jake wasn't louder than usual.

"Are you humming?" Alex says, after Jake gets set up at the reading table that Alex now thinks of as *his*. Alex isn't hovering. Hovering would mean he's interested. Annoyance is a form of interest, Alex tells himself.

Jake gives him a sheepish smile, and if Alex has spent the last week thinking about the *Jake Fischer smile taxonomy*, it's only because he's a librarian and librarians love to catalog. "Sorry," Jake says. Which doesn't answer the question.

Something in the noise gets a little quieter, like Jake consciously turned himself down. He reaches into his bag and retrieves a few books: one he borrowed from the library and a few that Alex doesn't recognize. He sets them out along with a set of highlighters in a clear plastic pack and a pack of those little tabby-flag things that make it a pain to prep books to be reshelved.

He looks like he's come for a long day of reading. Which means that he's not chasing ghosts. Which means Alex will have the assurance of having him here and not doing something foolish. Not that he was worried.

"That equipment work out okay?" Alex asks before he can stop himself.

Jake smiles up at him. "I'm still here, right? So yeah, it

worked out pretty well." As if his options are *mortal danger* and *at the library taking color-coded notes.*

"That stuff still work—the EVP-EMF things?"

"Yeah," Jake says, amusedly. "They still work."

"I found a file saying they're ten years old. Sometimes older electronics rust out."

"The previous owner knew how to take care of things."

Previous owner. That itch in Alex's brain is back, the one intensified by the bruising on Jake's knuckles, his hum like an atmosphere of static. *Do I know you?* Alex resists asking. He probably can't stand here all day staring at Jake—Alex brought crafts because today is crafts day, and Alex loves crafts day until he has to spend the afternoon scraping Elmer's glue off the tables.

"I'm going to get coffee," Alex says.

Jake nods, like he's expecting Alex to say more.

"Bye," Alex adds.

And Jake's laugh is especially loud given how quiet the library is.

BY MIDAFTERNOON, CRAFTS DAY IS IN FULL SWING. THIS ONE IS Halloween-themed. Each kid is decorating something that scares them, because social-emotional learning is important and because Alex spent the first eight years of his life scared that the sidewalk would spontaneously turn to quicksand until he found out that there were in fact much more frightening things.

Most of the kids have chosen ghouls or monsters, but one kid makes a bright orange circle with thick black stripes. Alex is about to ask if they're afraid of tigers when the kid taps their creation and whispers, "basketball."

Their babysitter slides up to Alex. "Gym class isn't going so well."

Alex asks if the kid wants to add fangs to his basketball and receives an outraged look.

"It's already scary," the kid says.

And Alex laughs.

After they make a nominal effort to clean up, he gathers everyone for a post-crafts story on the big rug with the letters and numbers and shapes. Most kids watch attentively. A few play with tufts of the rug. One naps and issues the occasional high childish snore. Alex doesn't always love his job—some days being underfunded and overworked means dragging himself home and not having the energy to crack a book—but if he believed in auras, right now his would be glowing contentedly.

He spends his time reading clearly but slowly, pausing to ask kids what they see in the book's illustrations, occasionally translating a word into Spanish. A noise gets his attention, like something enervating his jaw. When he looks up from the book he's reading, Jake is standing about ten feet back from the group. He has on that same sweater he had on when Alex met him, the cozy green one that makes his eyes somehow grayer. His bookbag sits heavy on his shoulder. His hands are stuffed in his pockets, the effect of which makes him look both handsome and regretful. When he catches Alex looking at him, he nods as if saying goodbye.

"See you tomorrow?" Alex calls to him. The assembled children look over. A few of their adults nudge each other as if Alex divulged something in the tone of his voice.

Jake's smile goes even sadder. "Here's hoping."

THE NEXT DAY WHEN ALEX ARRIVES AT THE LIBRARY, JAKE isn't there.

There's no real reason he should be. It's not like he's been there for ninety-nine point nine percent of the time Alex has worked here. Patrons come and go. They're supposed to. It's a lending library not a *stay in one place so I know you're not putting yourself in danger...library.*

Alex clearly needs coffee and a distraction. Fortunately, some of the books in the book drop are decorated with tabby flags. He could let a volunteer pick those out but he wants something to do with his hands that's not looking up where local ghost-hunting spots are and...he doesn't know. Finding Jake, somehow.

Here's hoping. What Jake said twice. Like he was banking his survival on something as flimsy as hope.

Alex can't control that, so he focuses his attention on picking out tabby flags and assembling them into a larger and larger ball. Here's a pink one annotated with an exclamation point. Here's a blue one with a heart drawn in highlighter. Alex doesn't have a huge reverence for books as physical objects—the first time he weeded the entire library collection disabused him of that. Libraries get "donations" in the form of moldy magazines and outdated textbooks and other detritus that people don't want to keep but are reluctant to reclassify as trash, as if doing so would render certain parts of their lives waste. But he doesn't really get going to the effort of carefully annotating a book only to dump it in a book drop. Then again, maybe the experience of reading a book is more important than the outcome of having read it.

By the time he's at the end of the book, he's glancing at the door every other pull of a tabby flag. He has other stuff to do. Jake will either come in or he won't. If he doesn't...he doesn't. They've barely had two conversations. Alex should not be concerned. Except he is.

Dammit.

He tosses the accumulated tabby flag ball into the trashcan then sits down at his computer and Googles *ghost-hunting spots Providence Rhode Island*. A bunch of sites pop up. Apparently, Providence is quote unquote *very haunted*. Where would Jake go—to a cemetery? To one of those roadside memorials with a small plastic cross? Was there a specific case he was tracking or was he just a ghost opportunist? And what happened to the ghosts when he caught them?

Alex carries those questions outside along with the sign declaring the library officially open for the day. Which is when he spots Jake's truck. It's parked off to the side, tucked in a particular inlet of the building that's more visible leaving it than entering it.

Great, he's alive. That should be enough to absolve Alex of his need to check on him. Jake's a grown man—a very tall grown man with a smile that's sharp at the edges and knuckles that imply he can hold his own in a fight. Alex should not be worried about him.

Dammit.

Alex marches over to the truck. It's an older model— dark green like Jake's sweater—and covered in a light film of dust. Jake is asleep in the front seat, slumped like he might have passed out from exhaustion. His hair has drifted onto his forehead. His eyelashes are a sweep on his cheeks. And—

Is that blood? Because he has something rust colored smeared down his jaw.

Before Alex can stop himself, he raps at Jake's window.

Jake startles awake. More accurately, he comes up

swinging as if he's used to leaving dream-space and winding up in the middle of a fight.

Alex should not be here, should not be worried. He raps again, less to wake Jake up and more to communicate the question sitting on his tongue: *Jake, what the fuck?*

After a second, Jake seems to register where he is. He blinks blearily at Alex, then rolls down the window. The truck has a bench seat, and he scooches himself sideways like he's concerned that he and Alex will accidentally collide. For a guy who clearly doesn't want Alex to touch him, he sure does come around a lot.

With the window down, it's clear that the smear on Jake's face is in fact blood—a few dried droplets scatter his cheeks like freckles.

"You okay?" Alex asks.

Jake frowns, then glances down at himself. And yeah, that blood smear extends down his shirt. "I'm great," Jake says, like he doesn't quite understand the question.

"You're bleeding."

"It's mostly stopped."

"*Mostly?* Right, either we're going to a hospital or you're going to tell me what's wrong."

"No hospitals," Jake says flatly. "And I found a ghost."

"What happened?"

"What usually happens. It threw me around the room for a while."

"And so you decided to sleep it off in my library parking lot?"

"It was..." Jake pauses for a moment like he's feeling for what he wants to say. "I knew I was safe here."

Safe. A word Alex is not going to let get to him, except for how it does. Jake was in danger, and he knew the library was safe. That *Alex* was safe.

"Fine." Alex steps back, enough that Jake will have space to open the door.

"Fine, what?" Jake calls.

"Come in and get cleaned up. There's a first aid kit you can use."

"Alex, you don't have to—"

"How did you know my name—that first time we met?"

"It was on your lanyard."

Alex examines his work badge, which does in fact say *Alex* in big letters and *Angelides* in much smaller ones. "You said my last name correctly. Most people would say *Angel-ides* not *Angle-ides*."

"Which is it?" Jake asks.

"*Angle-ides*."

"Huh. Must have been a lucky guess." Even though Jake says it with a knowing tilt in his voice. He opens the truck door, then descends gently onto the parking lot asphalt. In the morning light, it's obvious there's a bruise forming under the blood smear.

"You look like shit," Alex says.

"Thanks! I feel like shit too." But Jake laughs.

Alex leads him into the library, back to the staff kitchen that holds a well-stocked first aid kit, even if the only things Alex usually needs from it are Band-Aids and Narcan.

There's no great place to do this. The bathrooms are all single-stall and their only flat surface are the baby-changing tables. Alex also doesn't want Jake to get blood on his kitchen. "One of the study rooms has a busted camera," he says. "You can clean up in there."

Jake follows him down the hallway to the study room housing a long, scratched-up wooden table and a bulletin board advertising opportunities to work part-time for the local historical society. A single camera is mounted in the corner, its lens coated in black spray paint.

Alex would almost admire the vandal's efforts to stick it to the surveillance state if he didn't also have to put in a maintenance ticket that'll take months to fill. "See." He points to the camera. "Busted."

Jake sets down his bag on the table. From it, he pulls a pack of wet wipes and a rolled-up T-shirt. He looks back at Alex and, yeah, Alex should probably give him some privacy. Even if Jake slides off his winter coat, followed by his green cardigan, then finally strips off his T-shirt.

In his clothes, it's easier to hide his size. Out of them... Jake's shoulders are broad; his back tapers to a narrow waist. He's the kind of lean that's a world's distance from *skinny*, muscular enough that he must either work at it or need to be that way for whatever it is he does.

Alex isn't staring. Or if he is, it's only because of the scars crisscrossing the pale olive skin of Jake's back. Some are fresh, some faded. A particularly pronounced one runs around the join of his elbow like train tracks. *Who did that to you?* Alex bites back, then mentally revises. *What did that to you?*

Jake extracts a wet wipe from the package of them, then begins rubbing himself down in an efficient set of circles. For a guy who flinched when Alex touched him, Jake doesn't seem to have a problem with Alex watching him take a shirtless wet-wipe bath.

Alex should go. His feet don't seem to get the message, remaining stubbornly on the floor. This wouldn't be the first time Alex lost an argument to himself, especially one he's not fully committed to.

Especially when Jake cranes his head back. His hair falls

across his forehead. He offers Alex the laziest version of his smile. "You making sure I'm okay?"

"It's hard not to," Alex replies, then clarifies, "with all the blood, I mean. I take it this isn't your first ghost-hunting rodeo."

Jake's eyebrows rise.

"The scars on your back."

"Oh yeah," Jake says. "Definitely not my first ghost-hunting rodeo."

Ghosts aren't real, but Alex doesn't think Jake could do that much damage to himself over that many years without chasing *something*. Whatever it is, he seems like he needs a friend. Which is why Alex says, "When do you go out hunting again?"

Jake's eyebrows go up even farther. "Probably tonight."

Tonight. Not even a break to let his wounds heal. Alex shouldn't be worried about him. Jake is a library patron about whom Alex should be officially neutral. Except for the casual way Jake accepted the blood on his face, the bruising on his knuckles, Alex's clear attention. A tug in Alex's gut, one that Alex usually ignores, says *this way*, as if Alex has no choice but to follow.

So the words slide out. "If you're going out," Alex says, "take me with you."

For a second, Jake looks like he's going to say no. That he'll shake his head and that will be that. Worse, he might say *yes*, and that'll leave Alex to do what—go on a wild ghost chase with a man who came into his library good-naturedly bruised up?

"Are you sure?" Jake asks, as if Alex simply misspoke.

No. "Why not?"

"I thought you didn't believe in ghosts or ghost-hunting," Jake says.

"I don't. Not the first one anyway."

"If that's the case, why do you want to come?" Jake smiles again, another of those lazy smiles, though his eyes are assessing.

Because I'm afraid of what'll happen if I don't, Alex doesn't say. That would be uncomfortably close to caring, a step out of neutrality into someplace far more dangerous. "Any library patron is entitled to use that equipment. Including me."

That gets Jake to laugh. "Fine. But we're gonna do the easy version."

"Wimpy ghosts?" Alex asks.

Jake's smile goes tight, then he shakes his head. "No such thing."

3
____

ALEX SPENDS THE REST OF THE DAY WONDERING IF HE SHOULD cancel, especially since Jake's version of *easy* ghost-hunting is apparently hanging out in a cemetery for much of the night while various meters and recorders do most of the work.

All that's waiting for Alex back at Sofia's is a half-finished book and a half-empty bed. So he doesn't cancel.

Jake assures him that he'll be back at the library before Alex's shift is over. It's probably not chill for Alex to look out the window every five minutes during his last hour of his shift, but that's what he does. Jake's truck rolls up at five minutes to five. Alex waves to the librarian who's covering closing, then pulls on his coat, wondering if he should bring anything but himself and his phone and his apprehension that's slowly morphing into something else that might possibly border on excitement.

Whatever he's feeling must show, because when he goes to the passenger side of Jake's truck and levers himself in, Jake says, "And I thought your face would crack."

"What?"

"You're almost smiling."

Alex rearranges his face into even more of a scowl mostly to watch Jake laugh and slap his hand on the steering wheel. He looks better than he did eight hours ago: showered, in clean clothes. He has on a sweater—a gray one that makes his eyes look even greener. The collar slips a little, revealing the glint of a necklace.

All of which only throws the big-ass bruise on his cheek into clearer relief.

"How's the face?" Alex asks.

"Better. I spent most of today icing it at my apartment."

My apartment and not *home*, and Alex doesn't quite know what it's like to have that as a distinction, since he moved into Sofia's house when he was eight and never really left.

Still, if Jake has a place to lay his head… "How come you came to the library last night and not there?" Alex asks.

That makes Jake shift around. He puts the truck in gear, checks his mirrors, checks them again. People who carry their own set of highlighters aren't usually reckless drivers, but something Alex's stomach settles when Jake grips the wheel at a perfect 10 and 2 o'clock, then slowly begins to navigate out of the library lot and onto the street.

"Ghosts sometimes follow me off a job," Jake says, finally, as he makes his way through Providence rush hour traffic. "If there's a place that they know to avoid, then I'll stay there for a while to throw them off the trail."

"Ghosts don't like libraries?" Alex asks, semi-affronted.

Jake laughs. "Everyone likes the library, right?"

"I mean, yeah?"

This time, Jake's laugh fills the truck, and Alex gets a strange flash of déjà vu. *We've done this before.* Except of course they couldn't have.

Jake taps the steering wheel a few times as if he's

deciding what to say. "Ghosts want to tell their stories. When you have a lot of other competing stories—books, but also other people—they don't like that very much."

"So the library's too noisy?" Alex teases.

"Kinda. More like when you're at a library, you get a sense of a community, right? All the people there and the books they pick out and what stories they choose to tell themselves. Most ghosts are selfish. I get it. They don't have anyone to talk to so when they do, they're pretty fucking loud. But at the library, they can't be the only voice in the room."

It takes Alex a minute to process that, both the information and that Jake feels the same way about libraries that he does—how they're so much more than a building that holds books.

Jake doesn't seem to mind the silence. He taps his fingers against the wheel, realigns his phone where it's clipped to a dashboard holder to display directions.

"So what happens," Alex says, "when ghosts get to say what they want to say?"

"Usually, they depart to the great spooky beyond or whatever." Jake lifts his hand from the wheel long enough to do wiggly fingers. Then his expression turns more somber. "And I hold onto those stories for them."

Which would explain Jake's *hum* like a thousand voices sunk into his skin. Even if, in the truck, that hum is quieter. A purr, possibly, something almost contented. "Oh, we're here." Jake pulls his truck into an open parking space on the street. "That was quick."

Here is a small cemetery that's surrounded by a low stone wall and a wrought iron fence. Jake hops out of his truck and pulls several bags from the back seat. One of them is a black waterproof gear bag of the kind Alex expected for this trip. The other is a large brown paper bag that he hands to Alex, careful to avoid their fingers brushing. "I ordered dinner. I didn't know if you were a vegan or had other stuff you wouldn't eat, so I got a couple options."

Alex isn't a vegan anymore: he was for a while, but it didn't take when Sofia got into cheesemaking. He tries to square Jake, who bought him dinner and casually inquired if he's vegan, with Jake, who flinches back from being touched.

Maybe the latter has more to do with Jake's general fastidiousness or the buzz of ghosts under his skin. The best thing to do is probably just ask, even if some part of Alex still expects to hear that it's because Alex is gay. "I get you're all..." Alex steps back to indicate the personal hula hoop of space Jake prefers. "But is it okay for me to help you out?"

Jake's forehead does a confused-wrinkle thing that Alex refuses to find adorable. "What?"

"It's fine if you don't want me to touch you. But if you get hurt, can I render aid?"

"*Render aid*," Jake repeats, then holds up a hand like he's asking for time.

Alex expects an automatic yes. Of course Alex can help out if Jake gets clobbered by a ghost. Of course he can put his first aid training to use.

Slowly, like he's been chewing on the question, Jake nods. "This bag has nitrile gloves in it." He taps the black gear bag. "I don't want you to..." he begins then trails off.

Hurt yourself? Touch me? Alex autofills.

"Gloves are better," Jake finishes.

Alex shifts the bag of food, which is warm like Jake picked it up right before he came to get him. As if this is more than two people who met randomly at a library hanging out in a graveyard. If Jake wants gloves, he can wear gloves.

"Got it," Alex says. "So, are we gonna meet a ghost or what?"

Meeting a ghost involves first getting into the cemetery through an iron gate that takes a few tries before the latch releases. "There's sometimes night security, but mostly the neighbors are just snoops," Jake says.

"You come here often?" Alex teases.

"Not really. It's historical, so most of the ghosts have already said their piece and scooted on. But it kind of has sentimental value." Though Jake doesn't clarify what that value is as he holds the gate open to admit Alex.

Inside, the cemetery is quieter than the surrounding neighborhood. Outside it was the particular damp of mid-October New England. Here it's atmospheric. They make their way down a paved path to a low platform that's been built into one of the lawns. "They stage some of the restoration equipment on this to keep it out of the mud," Jake says, at Alex's questioning look. "Also makes for a good place to camp out."

At that, Jake begins what Alex can tell is a well-practiced process. First, he wipes down the platform with a towel. Then he lays out a small tarp. Then he pulls out various pieces of equipment—the EMF and EVP and flashlight and a notebook that he flips to a new page.

"What time is it?" he asks, and Alex tells him.

"Would you say this is more foggy or misty?"

"What's the difference?"

"Right, mist-fog." Jake's pen scratches across the paper.

Alex peers over the notebook page to see what he's writing. Given the difference in their height, he has to go up on his toes, close enough at Jake's elbow that he can almost feel the heat of him and the soft puffs of his breath.

Jake has inevitably good handwriting, a clearly ordered way of taking notes. Most of what he's writing are details about the location, the visibility conditions, the weather.

Except on its own line, there's *Companion: Alex Angelides* with little hatch marks around it for emphasis like this is something Jake wants to remember. He smiles when he catches Alex snooping, then tucks the pen back into his notebook. "Right," Jake says, "let's eat."

The food turns out to be Chinese takeout—dumplings, egg rolls, vegetarian lo mein and beef with broccoli. After they eat, Jake withdraws a blue and white box of donuts from his bag.

Alex picks them up and examines the box. "Impulse buy?"

"Nah. They're what my family always eats at funerals. A friend of mine used to joke that we were always at a lot of funerals—just late." Jake says it the same way he said *sentimental*, with a regretful twist to his expression.

So Alex takes a donut, and they sit for a while, chewing side by side. There's something familiar about this, the same way there was in the truck. Jake might have issues with skin-to-skin contact, but he doesn't flinch back from the brush of Alex's coat sleeve against his shoulder.

And Alex doesn't think many homophobes bring queer librarians on dinner-and-a-ghost-show dates. *If it's not that...* He looks up to find Jake studying him with that same look he had on during library reading time, like there's something fascinating between the threads of Alex's eyelashes or among his late-evening stubble.

After a second, Jake shakes his head like he's clearing a thought. "Hope you enjoy being bored."

Even if Alex really isn't bored, not when Jake's shoulder brushes his again. "What do you mean?"

"Sometimes ghosts show, sometimes they don't. These ones are old enough that we might be getting some faint pickups on the EVP but not much more than that. Just don't get your hopes up."

My main hope is you making it out of here alive. "What do you usually do to pass the time?"

"A bunch of stuff. Music, audiobooks. I did crochet for a while if you can believe it."

Alex imagines him sitting alone all night with only a hook and skein of yarn for company. It's enough to make him glance at Jake's hands with their long, quick fingers that Alex, contrarian that he is, wants to touch. It's been a long time since he fantasized about holding someone else's hand. If he concentrates hard enough, he can envision the thrum of Jake's pulse, the slight widening of his eyes in shock or delight. Alex leans forward, weight on his elbows, like he's reminding himself he shouldn't. "Why'd you stop crocheting?" he asks.

Jake's shrug brushes his shoulder against Alex's. "Didn't have anyone to really make things for. It was easier when I had someone else to go hunting with."

Something about *someone else* makes Alex's stomach tighten. Another companion, whose name got written in Jake's notebook. "What happened to them?" Alex asks.

Jake gives him another of those indecipherable looks. "He and I drifted apart. You ever have one of those fights that's not *really* about the fight but about all the other stuff you're not saying?"

Which sounds like it's less about fights Alex has had

over the years so much as about a very specific fight. "Bad friend breakup?"

Jake shakes his head. "Not exactly. More like—" But Jake doesn't finish the sentence. Not when the EMF reader kicks from chatter to scream. Alex's hands go reflexively to his ears while Jake twists the knob down to a more manageable —but not quiet—volume.

"We got one?" Alex says over the din.

"We definitely got one."

"What do we do now?" Something in Alex is already kicking into gear, as if fight, flight, or freeze has a fourth component: telling a ghost to fuck off. Alex's hands itch for a book, the right book that will tell him what to do. As it is, when Jake hands him something, he accepts it.

Until he realizes it's a taser. "Jake, what the fuck?"

Jake laughs. "It mostly just acts as a deterrent to them. They're already dead, remember?"

"Right. Right." Even if the taser sits heavy in Alex's hands. "Shouldn't we just ask it about its unfinished business?"

Jake's smile goes indulgent, but he shakes his head. "I tried that. Some hunters can do that—the real intuitive ones, at least."

"What works now?"

"I guess we're gonna find out." And he turns to where the ghost is barreling down on them from across the cemetery.

Alex wasn't entirely sure what a ghost looks like— absurdly, he thinks of a kid in a white ghost costume or possibly a basketball with fangs. This one is a slightly too thick clump of mist, one moving faster than Alex can really process.

"Sorry," Jake says.

And Alex doesn't have time to ask *Sorry for what?* before Jake grabs him by the shoulders and sends them both toppling off the platform. They end up next to each other in the soft grass, Jake's hand against the center of Alex's chest.

"Stay down," Jake breathes, low. "Ghosts can't see too well. Sometimes they're charging you and just kind of miss. Think quiet thoughts."

Mostly Alex is thinking about the firm pressure of Jake's palm and the smile in his voice and how his lips are very close to Alex's ear. Mortal danger feels a lot like being twenty-three again—equal parts terrifying and exciting.

After a few long minutes, during which the condensed water on the grass starts to seep into Alex's socks, the EMF quiets. Jake shifts his hand, withdrawing it carefully from Alex's chest, then sits up. A few blades of grass are stuck in his hair. His necklace—a silver chain with a large star of David pendant on it—has slipped out from his shirt collar. But what gets Alex's attention isn't those—it's the bright laughter of Jake's mouth and the way he wants to fit his hands around Jake's bruised face and kiss him.

Jake must catch him looking. "Just like old times, huh?" And he must be talking about someone else, some other *companion* who'd spent their evenings beside him, because he realizes his mistake. His smile fades. He pulls himself to standing as Alex does the same. Jake's necklace gets tucked back in, but there's still grass in his hair.

Alex wants to brush it out, if only to make his smile return. "You have..." Alex mimes scrubbing his own hair.

"Oh." Jake combs his fingers through his hair to dislodge the grass, then reseats himself on the platform. "Thanks."

"Think the ghost is gone?"

"Nope, not with all that wrought iron keeping it in here."

Jake gestures to the fence surrounding the cemetery. "Probably just regrouping."

"Did you want to split up to look for it?" Alex asks, even as he sits down next to Jake.

Jake gives him a horrified look. "Absolutely not. Stay close, okay?"

"Yeah." Alex nudges his shoulder companionably against Jake's. "I can do that."

After a second, Jake nudges him right back.

"You sure it didn't just leave?" Alex asks after they've been waiting for more than an hour. The EMF meter plays its familiar chatter. Every twenty minutes or so, Jake reviews the EVP's recordings, but thus far hasn't heard anything more interesting than the traffic or the background patter of rain.

"Told you this meant being okay with being bored," Jake says.

I'm not bored. Bored would imply that Alex is having a bad time, which he isn't. Not when they've spent most of the hour trading horror stories—in Alex's case, library patron horror stories, in Jake's case, literal ones—back and forth. In that time Alex has learned that Jake is from Maryland, that he grew up in the "dull" suburbs, that he went to but didn't graduate from college because "the ghost stuff kind of took over," and that he does not bat any of his considerable eyelashes in disbelief when Alex mentions his aunts.

Alex always has to weigh how far into meeting someone new to mention his family. Beyond homophobia, people have things to say about adopted kids, beginning with "do you ever miss your real family?" as if that's something that shouldn't get you socked in the mouth.

So he tries for the briefest version of things: Car accident. Foster care. Adoption.

Jake's lips turn down at the edges, and Alex wonders if he should change the subject. If this isn't really a *first date* conversation, even if this isn't a date. Until Jake drops a hand on Alex's knee, a brief tap of reassurance that nevertheless makes Alex glance down at the long curl of Jake's fingers around his kneecap before Jake withdraws his hand.

Over the years, Alex has found that there's no real great segue out of *my dad died in front of me*, so is about to say, *So tell me about that gnarly scar on your elbow* when the ghost comes back.

This time, they don't get the warning of the EMF meter. A clump of mist coalesces beside them and then opens its mist-mouth and expels what Alex can only classify as a terrifying screech.

Jake immediately begins rooting through his bag. "Hold it off."

Alex is about to ask *how* when, right, the taser. He activates it and sends a crackle through the mist, which hisses its objections and splits and reforms a few feet back as if chastened. He does it again, this time with more confidence, poking the taser through like he's drilling holes through the ghost's body and getting the gratification of its wail.

The third time, though, Alex gets overconfident: he shoves the taser at the ghost, which screams and parts and reforms around his arm. Pain shoots up through Alex's forearm, a freezing-burning sensation he hasn't felt since he was twelve and wanted to see if you could burn yourself by putting ice and salt on your skin, one of the few times Sofia ever yelled at him for endangering himself.

"*Fuck.*" Alex's fingers loosen around the taser, but if he drops that, he won't have anything to defend them with—himself or Jake.

Jake's still digging in his bag. "I'm going, I'm going." Said more to himself than to Alex.

So Alex grips the taser tighter and ups its output. "Get the fuck back," he says with all the authority he wielded when he used to bounce punk shows.

The ghost gets back, only as far as the extension of Alex's arm. Alex's muscles have already begun to shake—stress, adrenaline—and he doesn't know how much longer he can do this for.

"Finally," Jake says, pulling something out of the bag, a clear glass sphere the size of a baseball. He sits himself down on the tarp, cross-legged, holding the ball between his palms. "Now don't freak out."

"Why would I—" Alex begins.

Then Jake's eyes go a milky, ghostly white.

A wave, not quite a sound, ripples out from Jake, then reverberates through the cemetery around them. Jake is conscious, at least, judging by him chanting in a language that Alex doesn't recognize, smooth, except for the occasional *ch* in the back of his throat.

Whatever he's saying, the ghost must not like it, because the mist roils and condenses like it's angry. A few times, it swoops toward Jake only to retract itself as if sensing it's in danger. At least Alex hopes it's in danger.

Alex waves the taser again, but stops when Jake pauses chanting. He flicks his fingers as if beckoning the ghost. "Let it come." Then goes back to chanting. The glow in his eyes brightens like twin candles, like a lure, until finally, finally, the ghost starts funneling toward him in a neat line as if drawn through a straw.

Alex breathes a sigh of panicked relief and he's about to declare victory—their first ghost!—when Jake whispers, "Oh shit."

Then goes limp.

The sphere rolls out of his hands and across the platform in a series of thunks that Alex doesn't think he'll ever be able to unhear. Jake's eyes shift from milk white to an awful watery blue. The rest of his body lolls to one side, arm drooping over the edge of the platform. If Alex didn't know better, he'd think Jake was asleep. Or worse.

Alex tucks the taster into his coat pocket then drops to his knees, almost but not quite bringing his hands to Jake's face. Gloves. Right. He promised he'd wear gloves. He digs through the bag and quickly realizes why it took so long for Jake to find that glass ball—the bag has a thousand interior pockets, none labeled.

"When we get through this," Alex grouses, "I am cataloging that thing."

Finally, he finds a set of purple nitrile gloves in a small plastic bag. He slides them on, then turns his attention back to Jake, who hasn't moved. Who, other than the faint ventilation of his breath, isn't moving.

Alex doesn't know anything about ghost-related first aid, but he does do CPR training every few years. He taps Jake's arm. Gives a firm, "Hey, bud, you okay?"

No response.

"Jake." His voice sounds thin. "Wake up."

No response.

There's something horrifying about this stillness. Around them, the city continues its pace. Traffic shushes through the streets. The mist coalesces into rain.

He taps Jake again on his arm, then his cheek, then rolls him over to the prone position, as if Jake is merely ill and

Alex has summoned an ambulance. Most of his first aid training centers around how to keep a person breathing until someone with better training arrives.

Now there's no one else coming and Alex doesn't know what to do.

"Jake," he pleads, "snap out of this."

He begins patting Jake down to find anything—a medic alert bracelet, an emergency contact—anything that will tell him what to do when this happens. They probably should've exchanged *that* information and not funny stories or the details of Alex's whole deal, even if it was nice to talk to someone who didn't respond with pity or scorn.

The glow in Jake's eyes flickers. Alex doesn't know if he's winning or losing whatever battle he's in. If he's hearing about the ghosts' small triumphs and petty jealousies or if he's getting his ass kicked the one place Alex can't come in swinging to protect him.

"Jake," Alex says, desperately. He doesn't know what else to add.

Jake gives a huffing breath in response. Dark lines start creeping along his face and jaw. Underneath those, his skin goes ashen. He wheezes like he's being choked and that's it, Alex doesn't know what he's supposed to do, but he needs to do *something*. Jake's coat pockets yield nothing better than a pack of tissues. His pants pockets produce his keys, his wallet, his phone, and a tube of cherry ChapStick, the kind Alex buys when he's feeling nostalgic but he's not exactly sure what for.

His phone is of course locked. Alex hovers it over his face to see if the face recognition will unlock it and gets prompted to enter a lock code. That won't work. Maybe it's the kind that opens with a fingerprint. He picks up one of Jake's hands in his, trying to press the pad of his left index finger to the lower part of the screen when the bare skin of his wrist brushes the bare skin of Jake's.

Oh fuck.

Whatever Alex expected to happen—an explosion, Jake waking to chastise him—neither does. Instead he gets an acute sensation on the interior of his wrist, like sparks, like familiarity.

Jake doesn't stir. His eyes go even paler, like something within him has dimmed. None of this feels quite real: not the mist, not the ghost, not the glow of Jake's eyes or the lines infecting their way under his skin. They're darker now, like vines squeezing the life out of him from within. His breathing goes shallower, less even, until finally...it stops.

For a second, Alex doesn't know what to do. If he's going to be left in a graveyard with the corpse of a stranger who could have been a friend. Panic overtakes him. He kicks it away stubbornly. No, that's not what's going to happen. Jake is not going to die. *Fuck that.*

Alex strips off Jake's coat and pushes up his sweater and T-shirt to his armpits to reveal his chest and abdomen. There are more scars here, some faded with time, like Jake's been doing this for years. Something clenches in Alex's chest. He thinks of Jake, injured, driving someplace he knew he could pass out safely. The exhaustion under his eyes and the joy in them when he was telling Alex to think quiet thoughts.

The second Jake wakes up Alex is going to yell at him to be more careful.

Alex rubs his gloved knuckles down the line of Jake's sternum, feeling for his breath. None comes. Technically, he should do chest compressions first, but they didn't cover ghostly possession in Alex's CPR class, so he decides to wing it. He pinches Jake's nose shut, tilts his chin back to lengthen the line of his already-long neck. If this was at the library, they have a mask specifically for rescue breaths. All Alex has is his own slightly chapped lips and the fear that this won't work and the hope that it just might.

So he takes a deep inhale, and presses his lips to Jake's, and breathes.

CPR is nothing like a kiss. Nothing, except for the warmth of Jake's mouth under his and a shock like they've done this before, like some echo of a memory that Alex can't place, one that swims just below the surface of his consciousness. Alex breathes once, twice, then steels himself to begin chest compressions, to call 9-1-1 and damn the consequences. And he's about to pull his phone from his pocket, to put *the authorities* on speaker, when Jake shudders back to life.

He breathes like he's resurfacing, like he's struggling against some great and unseen current. Slowly, the black lines recede. The blue glow of his eyes transitions to a milky white and finally, finally, back to their familiar gray-green.

And Alex wants to kiss him again, to wrap his arms around him and hold him safe from the world, but he settles for the next best thing: punching him lightly in the arm and saying, "Jake, I'm going to fucking kill you."

Jake laughs wearily. "Where'd that ball get to—the glass one?"

It's not on the platform, so Alex has to root around for it. It's apparently hard to spot a transparent sphere on wet grass in the dark, but he does, then hands it to Jake and waits while Jake fills it with a ghostly glow.

After, Jake slumps as if that drained the last of his effort. And he's pale enough and weak enough that Alex picks up the coat he stripped off him and settles it across his shoulders.

For a second, they breathe together, Alex holding his coat around him, Jake looking up at him with an unreadable expression. He snakes a hand between them and touches something on Alex's face, the rough catch of his calluses a shock against the skin right below Alex's eye. He taps Alex's face like he's wiping away moisture. "I didn't mean to scare you," Jake says softly.

"You did."

Jake pulls back to study him. "For what it's worth, I'm sorry."

"It's okay."

"No, it's really not." Jake looks down, a sweep of his eyelashes against his cheek and they're close, close, close, in a way that makes Alex want to seal his mouth back over his and kiss him just to reassure himself that they're both still breathing. "It won't take long now," Jake says.

What won't? Then blackness begins to fizzle at the edges of Alex's vision, slowly, then all at once, darkness like a sudden curtain. The last thing he hears before he passes out is Jake's whispered, "I really am sorry."

4

———

Alex comes to and immediately wishes he didn't. His body hurts like he got thrown in a mosh pit at age thirty-four. The ceiling above him is a blank unforgiving white. He stares at it until his eyelids tire out. Where is he? And where's Jake? And what the fuck happened?

He manages to prop himself up on his elbows but gets no farther. Wherever Jake is, now Alex really *is* going to kill him. Just as soon as he can get to his feet.

For now he's stuck in a bedroom of what must be a rental. The décor is as impersonal as a hotel room, if somewhat shabbier. A few of Jake's things are scattered atop one of the dressers. A pile of library books from Alex's library. The glass sphere.

A black velvet necklace box that Alex knows is Jake's because Alex bought it for him. Ten years ago. When they knew each other.

When they were *hunting companions* and more than that. Until *something* happened and Alex spent a decade getting a master's degree and organizing community read-a-thons and Jake apparently kept hunting.

Alex's memories are still patchwork, still filling back in like something fuzzy on the edge of his vision got thrown into sharp relief. Questions fill his mind: If Jake obviously still remembered, was he just *messing* with him? Was this a prank? A second chance with Alex as an unsuspecting dupe?

As if on cue, Jake appears at the doorway, holding a mug and wearing an expression like he knows he's about to get yelled at.

Alex will not yell. For now. He sits up a little more and doesn't hide his grunt of discomfort. Jake winces—but he doesn't immediately apologize either.

"Is this your place?" Alex asks.

"Yes."

"How'd you get me back here?"

Jake's mouth goes tight. "Carefully."

"How long have I been here?"

"Better part of a day."

"Fuck." Alex gropes around, unsure of where his clothes got to. He's still in the T-shirt and boxers he wore to the library, but his sweater and pants are gone. "Where's my phone?"

Jake hands it to him. On it, a dozen texts, some from his aunts and cousin, some from the library, all asking the same thing: where the hell is he?

"You could have woken me up." Alex can't keep the anger out of his voice. At Jake having done this and now standing here like he's expecting Alex to forgive him.

That Alex remembers from ten years ago: Jake putting himself in danger. When he survived, he'd turn to Alex and grin like he just got away with something. For a while, Alex found it charming. Now, definitely not. Alex composes a text and copies and pastes it into several chats. *Got sick last night and crashed with a friend. Sorry, should have let you know.*

His boss at the library replies with an *Are you okay?*

His cousin sends a *"sick"* in quotation marks like she knows something else is going on.

Sofia, perhaps from psychic powers or more probably just because she's known him his entire life, says, *Which friend?*

Which only adds another question to Alex's endless list of them: If Sofia knew about Jake and, if so, why she kept all this from him.

While Alex was texting, Jake receded back to the doorway. He's twisting his hands like he's washing them, like he's nervous to be called to account for all of this.

Alex has had a decade's practice at pruning back his temper. Red flicks at the edges of his vision, an anger that almost—*almost*—makes him forget the ache in his body or how Jake lied to him. How by standing in the doorway and not offering an immediate explanation, he's still lying.

All of which must play across his face because Jake gives him a searching, apologetic look. "You remember?" Jake asks.

As if Alex can pack a decade's worth of memory loss into those two words. "Yeah," he grits out, "I remember."

Jake goes to his dresser and searches in one of the drawers before he finds something and hands it to Alex: a white envelope with fingerprint dents already marring its surface, like it's been passed between hands for a decade. Dents Alex adds to as he grips it. Especially when he reads the name scrawled across the front—*Alex*. Written in his own handwriting.

"You told me to make sure you got this," Jake says.

Alex turns the envelope over a few times. It's old enough

the glue has hardened, the paper gone brittle. He wonders if he'll open it and find only dust. No, ten years usually isn't enough to crumble paper, but anything can turn to powder if it's mishandled. The way he feels right now. Like he might fracture into a thousand pieces.

Whatever his past self wanted him to know has waited ten years. It can wait a few more minutes. "What have you been doing?" he asks.

Jake's eyebrows creep toward his hairline in surprise. "Today?"

"For the past decade. Since we…" *Left each other?* "Since the last time we spoke."

For a second, Jake doesn't say anything. Alex understands that struggle. Mostly, when people ask what he's been up to, he has one of two options: a deep dive into the municipal politics of library funding or "not much." Especially when that question is really asking about his personal life. Most people don't want to hear about failed Grindr dates or the point at which having high standards becomes erecting walls.

Jake still hasn't said anything. Maybe he won't. Maybe he, like Alex, can't sum up ten years spent apart, and it was foolish to ask him to try.

"Mostly," Jake says finally, "I've been hunting ghosts and trying not to die."

"Like today?"

"I didn't say I was good at it."

You're still here. That's something ten years can't erase: Jake's absolute stubbornness. How he seemed easygoing, but every challenge just made him dig his heels in more. It's enough to make Alex insert the tip of his index finger under the envelope flap and slowly pry it open.

Inside, there's only a single piece of lined paper, edged

in soft perforation like it was torn from a notebook. The note on it is also written in Alex's handwriting, in the block letters he still favors because they make writing signage at the library easier.

Alex,

Whatever Jake needs, give it to him.

Alex

Alex reads it, then reads it again. He turns it over, holds it up to the light, like the rest of the message was written in lemon juice the way he taught his cousin to write in invisible ink when she was a kid. "That's it?"

"You were always pretty succinct." Jake says it almost like a joke. Like they can *joke* about this.

Alex grinds his back teeth together in an effort not to yell. "Tell me what's going on."

At that, Jake nods. He seats himself at the other end of the bed, near Alex's feet. "We used to hunt together ten years ago," Jake says.

"Yeah, I got that."

"We had a...disagreement. You wanted to quit hunting. So you asked me to hold onto those memories. Yours, some of Sofia's, a few other people's. I can because of—" Jake gestures down the line of his body as if to indicate his powers. "It was hardest with you. We spent so much of that year together and..." He trails off, then looks down at his hands stationed on his knees. "You asked me to take your memories, so I did."

And Alex doesn't know what's worse: to be the only person who remembers something or to not remember it at all. "What changed?"

"You told me that if I ever *really* needed something, I could come find you."

"You couldn't have just said all that?"

Jake gives him an incredulous *Jake* look like Alex has dared to tell him how to go about his business. Another memory snaps back into place: of Jake doing the same thing across a picnic table spread with an old map, enough that Alex jumped the table to stand on one of its attached benches, to peer down at Jake from newfound height and kiss the pretended outrage from his mouth.

His chest throbs, from the ache of the recovered memory—from missing that younger version of himself who's been gone for a decade, who was definite and driven and *in love*. That he remembers and, for a flash of a second, he wishes he couldn't.

Across the bed, Jake's mouth draws tight with tension. "What was I supposed to say to you? *Hey hot librarian guy, did you know we used to be friends? Like a long time ago? And we put ghosts to rest and also used to...*" His Adams apple bobs as he swallows. "I wanted to give you the opportunity to tell me to fuck off. If we went out hunting, I thought maybe it'd scare you and I could just let you go."

That thing in Alex's chest, the one that's ached since Jake walked into his library, gives another pang. "Well, that didn't work."

Jake laughs, then scrubs a hand over his face. "Yeah, it sure didn't."

"What happened when we—" Alex gestures between his lips and Jake's, and what he means is *CPR* but what he communicates is *we kissed*. He refuses to be embarrassed about that, not while lying in Jake's bed, wrung out, not while a strand of Jake's hair has fallen over his forehead and Alex's hands ache to push it away. To kiss him again, even if it's a kiss goodbye.

"I was holding your memories for you," Jake says. "And I guess I gave them back."

An *accident*. Something that's neither of their fault. Jake, who came back into his life just to give Alex the chance to walk away again. Alex, who wanted nothing more than to keep him safe. Alex laughs, unamused, and a sharp pain radiates through his side. He coughs to dispel it and only makes it worse.

"You should rest," Jake says.

Alex shakes his head. "There's one more thing you haven't told me."

"What's that?"

Alex sits himself up more in bed. His shoulders hurt from the memory transfer, from Jake hauling him around. Something just under his sternum aches too. That he remembers from the last time he and Jake were together: how Jake took his memories and told Alex to get moving so he didn't wind up in a motel room with Jake transformed into a stranger. The particular hurt of walking those twenty or so feet to his car. Then he got in it, adjusted his mirrors, and...nothing. Just mild confusion at what he was doing outside a motel in New York and exasperation at how bad traffic might be on the drive home.

Still, if ten years ago he trusted Jake enough to write himself that note, he should trust him now. Despite his trepidation, Alex's instincts agree. No, the message he's getting is clearer than instincts: a premonition. This is the correct path, no matter how stony. So Alex tries to keep the wariness from his voice as he says, "What's going on that you needed to come find me?"

JAKE DOESN'T TELL HIM, NOT IMMEDIATELY. FIRST, HE INSISTS on Alex making sure he's not injured, which leads to Alex stripping down in the glare of Jake's rented bathroom lighting. Alex was dreading shower slime or black mold, but the bathroom itself is clean—very clean.

When he calls that to Jake, who's hovering outside the door, Jake says, "Yeah, I'm working on that."

Alex does a cursory examination of himself and finds nothing worse than a few bruises, the product of having been lugged back to Jake's truck and then up the few steps to his apartment. Jake insisted this conversation required a rinse-off and a meal. By the time Alex runs the shower, which produces a sufficient amount of steam to fog up the bathroom, he doesn't disagree.

Alex gets in, then reaches out of the curtained tub to twist the bathroom doorknob to show it's unlocked. "If you want to come in," he calls.

And he expects Jake to let him be, but a minute later Jake knocks to announce his entrance. When Alex sticks his now-wet head out of the shower, Jake is carrying towels and a toothbrush still in a plastic wrapper.

"Thanks," Alex says.

"Least I could do." And Jake's smile has a tightness to it as he starts to leave.

"Wait!" Alex blurts. As soon as he's said it, he immediately starts regretting it—because there's no way to say *Please don't leave* without it sounding...needy. "Just, if you could stay in here. In case I collapse."

"Wouldn't want that." And Jake seats himself on the closed toilet.

Now that he asked him to stay, Alex probably needs to say something else. Conversation comes easy at work or in Sofia's garden, when there's the predictable rhythm of a year. Less so elsewhere, and he's not sure when his life became a commute between work and home without much flavor beyond the occasional hang out with friends. *Is this how you thought your life would turn out?* is a question Alex should probably save for when he isn't naked and slathering himself with Jake's soap.

"You okay in there?" Jake asks, after Alex hasn't said anything for a solid minute.

"Uh-huh."

"Water good?"

"Yeah, nice and hot."

"I got this place for the water pressure." There's a noise like Jake is shifting around.

"I'm still living at Sofia's," Alex admits. Because *yes, I still live with my adoptive aunts as an adult* has made more than one date look at him in pity.

"Oh yeah?" Jake says. "How is she?"

"Good. Place is too big for them to keep up by themselves. Plus, Sofia let me put a woodshop in the garage."

"You do carpentry now?"

"Yeah, got into it when..." When Alex was bored and couldn't remember how his life had been so full until abruptly it wasn't. "About eight years back."

"Have you made anything good?"

"A table, a few chairs. Other stuff. I ran out of people to give things to and didn't want to try selling it."

"Yeah, I know how that is." What Jake said about crochet —about how lonely it was to create something and have no one to give it to.

"I could make you some crochet hooks." The offer slips out before Alex can prevent it. He wishes he could take it back, could rid himself of that urge to *do* things for Jake—to watch him light up with thanks—as easily as the soap now sliding down the drain. "If you wanted."

"Do those take long?" Jake asks. A question that hides a

different one—if they'll even be talking to one another at the end of whatever this is.

"Don't know," Alex says. "I haven't made 'em before."

He cuts the water off, then stands, dripping, waiting for Jake to leave so he can grab a towel. Instead, there's motion at one end of the shower curtain—the towel being passed through. Alex plucks it from Jake, then pats himself off. He could just push back the curtain. It's not like they haven't seen one another naked. Those memories came back too— incandescently and all at once, and Alex shouldn't be thinking about semi-athletic sex he had at twenty-three at all but especially not when he's only a few feet from Jake and wearing only terrycloth.

Standing barefoot in the bathtub, the outline of Alex's body is probably visible through the double-layer of the curtain. He imagines Jake's disappointment: that he returned after a decade to find this current version of Alex, one that says *desk job* no matter how many weights he lifts.

But no, Jake said *hot librarian*. Like he looked at Alex, ten years older and softer, and liked what he saw. So Alex tucks the towel around his waist and pushes back the curtain.

Jake's still in the bathroom, rearranging something on the counter. He's studying his own reflection, a frown turning down the edges of his lips. Then he lifts his gaze to meet Alex's own in the mirror and smiles. "I brought you some clothes." Jake nods toward a pile of them. "Don't know if they'll fit."

"Yeah," Alex says, "I didn't get any taller."

Jake laughs at that, softly, but makes no move to leave. "You look okay."

"You mean, not mildly concussed from memory transfer?"

That gets another laugh, another assessing sweep that

Jake makes no effort to hide. "I meant you look good. Let me let you get changed." And he leaves, shutting the bathroom door with a quiet click.

Jake's clothes are too big on him. Alex has to roll the waistband of the sweats, which catch on the breadth of his thighs. The cuffs of Jake's long-sleeved T-shirt bunch at his wrists. Jake wasn't wrong to insist he got cleaned up: he does feel better after a shower. More able to process all of this, especially as he comes out of the bathroom and there's a sandwich waiting on a plate on the small kitchen table that Alex can barely squeeze himself under.

"How do you fit here?" Alex asks after his knees rap against table's underside again.

"Mostly, I eat on the couch."

"That doesn't bother you?" Because Alex remembers Jake having opinions about where food should be consumed: couches were okay for snacks but not meals, the car was anything goes, and the bed was an absolutely not. The fact of which Alex found out the first time he brought Jake breakfast in bed—from motel continental breakfast somewhere in the middle of Pennsylvania. Which seemed romantic at the time, in the way only a plastic cup of orange juice, a questionable bagel, and the feeling of being twenty-three and in love could be.

Alex bangs his knee against the table again. "Right, the couch." He transports his sandwich there, then pauses to examine it before he eats it. "Is this a chickpea sandwich?"

Jake shrugs, like that isn't the sandwich that Alex used to complain about never being able to find anywhere but cities. "It's just from the supermarket," Jake says. "But I have other stuff if you want to make something else."

"No, this works." And so Alex picks up his sandwich and eats, chewing on slightly stale multigrain bread along with the question: *After all these years, do you still miss me the same way I apparently miss you?*

After Alex has eaten and cleared and washed his plate, after Jake has swept the crumbs from his coffee table into his waiting palm and followed that with a cleaning rag, Jake says, "So, we should talk."

He's seated across from Alex on an oversized armchair that doesn't match any of his other furniture. As large as it is, Jake's knees still stick up.

I could make you a chair, Alex doesn't say. "Yeah, let's talk."

"Do you remember that house in Tarrytown?"

"You mean the one in north Yonkers?" But, yes, Alex remembers.

Their last job together. Smells can unlock memories, but now Alex has the opposite effect: a memory unlocks the wood-burning odor of a house fire, a scent followed by the acrid smell of burnt hair.

Ghost-hunting means making your peace with death, with knowing worst of people in all their greed and pettiness. These ghosts died in a house fire, an accident. No one's fault or negligence, just the cost of living in a time before building codes or fire suppression systems or even fire departments that weren't just your neighbors and a bucket line to the nearest river or well.

And so three boys and their parents were lost to the ashes.

Even with the benefit of ten years, Alex doesn't know why that house was the one that broke him. Jake walked out with tears tracking their way through the soot on his face and Alex said, *Stop hurting yourself like this.*

Jake shook his head. He claimed that all he needed was a meal and a good night's sleep, then picked his way through dinner. Later, Alex woke up in the middle of the night to find Jake sitting up on the other side of the bed, head in his hands. Neither of which was any different from the times it had happened before except how it was.

The next day, Alex quit.

Now Jake hasn't said anything. Maybe the same burning smell is filling his nose. Maybe he's waiting for Alex to tell him to go fuck himself. Alex could. The words are right there. *I don't want to watch you hurt yourself again*, followed by him stomping out of Jake's life.

Instead Alex says, "Why now?"

Jake's eyebrows go up.

"It's been ten years," Alex continues. "They died in, what, the 1700s?"

"Yeah."

"So why now?"

Jake takes a long inhale, like he knew the question was coming. Like he *prepared* with a bullet pointed index card and a rehearsal in front of a mirror.

And Alex remembers how they'd send Jake in to charm whichever landlord or floor supervisor or storeowner so that they could come in and de-ghost their structure. So Alex digs his fingernails into the cotton of his borrowed sweatpants and focuses on how much he doesn't want a polished *Jake Fischer* answer. "Tell me the truth. No *Jake* bullshit."

"Jake bullshit?"

"Don't pretend like you don't know."

From the smile playing at the corner of Jake's mouth, he absolutely does. "All right." Jake's shoulders settle. He gets that look of determination that Alex knows, one he missed in the last decade. "I can hear them," Jake says, softly, "and they're getting worse."

Dread coalesces in Alex's stomach. "Hear who?"

This time, Jake's smile is a sad one. "The boys. Sometimes their parents. They burned before anyone even knew the house was on fire."

"Can you hear them right now?" Alex asks.

Slowly, Jake nods. "It's faint. Usually it only got bad if I was in area. But in the past year, it's gotten worse. Sometimes I can't sleep because of it." He shrugs, a careless *Jake* what-can-you-do? shrug if not for the weariness in his shoulders.

A year. Alex can't imagine how that might slowly erode someone's sanity, can't imagine being woken in Providence by whispers across the water. How powerful their spirits must be to be heard like that—how powerful Jake must be to hear them.

"I'm not saying yes to the job," Alex says. A statement that comes with an autofill... *I'm not saying no either.* "But if I did, what would that involve?"

Jake's smile brightens minutely. "I've been doing some planning."

Of course he has. Jake loved to plan everything to the last detail. Loved just as much to shove that plan aside and improvise when things went wrong. How he'd turn to Alex, sweaty and grinning and say, *Some things you gotta do by feel.* Maybe that same impulse is what's keeping Alex sitting here. "Okay," he says. "What're you thinking?"

Jake's smile widens a fraction more. "Well, so glad you asked..."

So over the next hour, they talk.

A decade ago, Alex would have just thrown a toothbrush and a spare set of boxers in a bag and hopped in Jake's truck. At age thirty-four, he wants a plan. He wants hotel reservations and to know the last time Jake's truck got serviced and the state of his health insurance. None of which answers his real question: what happens if they don't succeed?

He texts his boss—*gonna need some time off*—and gets back a *good*, as if she was worried about him not using up his PTO. His cousin responds with a *steal a painting from the Met for me* when he says he's going to New York.

Sofia: where are you going?

Alex: tarrytown

Sofia: tarrytown or north yonkers?

"Does Sofia know?" Alex says, looking up from his phone.

Jake bites his lip. "Um."

"You said you took her memories. But it sure sounds like she knows."

"It's hard to hide something like this from a psychic."

"She's not..." Alex begins. *Actually psychic.* "That's just something she tells people to upsell tarot card readings."

"When I came back, you knew something was up, right?"

"I'm not psychic," Alex says, even if it sounds like a lie.

Jake hums at that, like he doesn't agree but is too polite to say so. "You always described it as this tug in your belly telling you to do something. Or not do it as the case may be."

The thing is, Alex does know, enough to predict which library volunteers will no-show. Enough that, when he used to play poker on Thursday nights, he got gently disinvited from the group after he kept winning. "Well, fuck."

Jake laughs, loud and delighted. "Yeah."

"Sofia must be better at it if she still remembers you."

Jake shrugs, a shrug that would look easygoing except for the tension lining his mouth. "You were pretty adamant that you didn't want anything to do with me. Sometimes that makes the whole thing easier. If people want to forget."

I'm sorry. Even if Alex isn't. He knew at the time it would be better to walk away. He wishes he was as certain now. He also still hasn't answered Sofia.

Alex: so you know what I'm doing

Sofia: yes

Alex: and you disapprove?

Sofia: I didn't say that

Even if Alex can sense it, as if disapproval could be carried across the city on cold wind. He sets down his phone and turns his attention to the map Jake has laid out on the coffee table, one that's marked with other hauntings in the Yonkers-Tarrytown area. "That's a lot of ghosts," Alex says.

"That place is supposedly the most haunted place in the country."

"You think that has something to do with why you can hear them?"

Jake frowns as he thinks it that over. "Maybe? I've sort of been avoiding that area. Felt like too big a job to tackle alone."

He doesn't say it particularly pointedly, but it slides under Alex's skin like a wood splinter. Jake's insinuation that Alex left him alone—not that Alex walked away hoping Jake would do the same.

"It's possible," Jake continues, "that all the ghost activity in the area is having a magnifying effect."

Alex leans over the map they've been examining, tracing

lines between each haunted site with his finger, feeling very much like he's about two seconds away from decorating a conspiracy board with red string, as he connects each haunting site into a chain, a spiral. A ghostly megaphone. No wonder Jake can't sleep.

Then a noise murmurs under the edge of his hearing. He almost mistakes it for the crinkle of a map. Until it happens again. Nothing else in the room is making a sound: just the drip of Jake's kitchen faucet echoing through the apartment and shallow cycling of Jake's breath.

When he looks up, Jake is studying him.

"They sound like paper," Alex whispers, in case the ghosts overhear and amplify their attack.

Slowly Jake nods. "They start out that way."

Start. Meaning whatever Jake's hearing is worse. "If I can hear them, so can Sofia."

Jake nods again.

Alex does a quick calculation of how many people there are in the tristate area, and what percentage of them might have latent psychic abilities. It comes out to a whole fuckton of people. "What do they want?" Alex asks.

Jake's smile is watery. "What everyone wants. To have their story told. Only they've been screaming for so long that—" He shuts his mouth with a click. "You can smell them burning up, right?"

Alex takes another inhale: smoke. "Yeah."

"Last night I was asleep on the couch. When I woke up my ceiling was smoldering."

Alex cranes his neck up. There's the tiniest dot of a black patch above his heard. *Fuck.*

"I know, there goes my security deposit, right?" Jake's laugh doesn't have much actual amusement in it. "So I want to give them some rest. Before they take me with them—along with everyone else."

Ten years ago, Alex chose to walk away from all this and told himself it was for both their benefit. Now he wishes his gut could tell him that he's doing the right thing for the right reason: to give old ghosts some peace and not to smooth the worried lines from the corners of Jake's eyes. None of that stops him from dropping his hands to the tops of his knees. "All right."

Jake's eyebrows rise. "All right?"

"I'll do it. The job."

"Why?"

That tug in Alex's belly lights up with equal parts apprehension—that this will end like it did ten years ago, with them parting as strangers—and hope. That maybe, just maybe, things will be different. "Just got that feeling, I guess."

5

———

EARLY THE NEXT MORNING, JAKE TEXTS THAT HE'S OUTSIDE Sofia's, ready to pick Alex up. Not that Alex needs the message—he's been waiting by the front door for almost twenty minutes.

Sofia drifts by, a mug of tea in hand, and he leans to hug her.

"I'll let you know when we get in," he says, like this is any other trip. Like it's normal to refer to Jake using a couple-ish *we* the way he might with another partner.

She draws back from him, then clutches her tea in one hand, her knuckles capped a tense white. "Be safe," she says, then amends. "Be as safe as you can."

He kisses her cheek, an action that brings him closer to the threads of gray in her hair. How many of those did he contribute to when he was a punk-ass kid? How many is he adding now? "I will," he says, then picks up his duffle.

Outside, Jake is sitting in his parked truck, bent over his phone screen. He puts the hazards on and hops out when Alex approaches, like he needs help shoving his bag in Jake's meticulously clean backseat.

Alex isn't sure if they're at the *hug in greeting* stage of reuniting—and he's not sure how those stages are altered by what might be the last job they ever do together—so he offers his approximation of a straight-guy one-armed hug and receives the briefest touch of Jake's clothed shoulder.

Up close, Jake smells like soap, toothpaste, and coffee, none of which is remarkable except his particular combination stirs something within Alex ten years in the making. How Jake's pillow smelled like that—how he'd return Alex's sweatshirts that he borrowed with that same scent clinging to the fibers.

"We should get going," Alex says hoarsely. Even if all they have ahead of them is a two-hour drive.

So he climbs into the passenger seat and reaches automatically to move the seat to his height. But of course it already is—Jake gave him a ride to the library so Alex could drive his car back to Sofia's.

There's something about that and about the second cup of coffee sitting in a cardboard tray and how Jake included two creamers even though Alex knows he doesn't drink coffee with them, and about how he waits for Alex to click in his seat belt before turning on the engine.

Something about all those things, and the way Jake's necklace gleams in the morning light, the same chain Alex bought him ten years ago when there was nothing they couldn't do.

Alex told himself he'd spend this trip only haunted by one thing—literal ghosts—but this feels like he's breathing life back into something almost, but not quite, snuffed out.

None of which he wants to put into words, so he settles for dropping his hand on the soft leather of the bench seat, inches from where Jake is resting his, but moving no closer.

"We going?" Alex asks, and Jake laughs and puts the truck in gear and drives.

THEY PULL INTO THEIR HOTEL PARKING LOT IN EARLY afternoon after stopping for lunch. They made good time, even if Alex secretly wishes for some kind of traffic snarl as an excuse to keep on the road. Ten years later, Jake has the same taste in music—*bad*—and the same loud laugh when Alex tells him just that.

Now Jake parks the truck, jumps out, stretches his legs. He's in a faded baseball hat, a white t-shirt with a puffer vest over it, a pair of gray sweatpants. All of which read *nondescript overage frat boy* to everything except Alex's brain, which is currently processing them as *nondescript overage frat boy porn*.

Jake looks over from where he's stretching. "I only booked one room if that's okay."

Alex swallows. "That's okay." It makes sense. One room means less money out of pocket. It also means Jake five feet away in the next bed. *Okay* is definitely what Alex is.

When they get inside, Jake smiles his way up to the clerk staffing the desk, gives his last name, and offers his credit card and photo ID.

"I hope you don't mind—" the clerk says.

Alex braces himself for one of any number of possibilities, including that the room they booked might only come with one bed.

"Housekeeping isn't quite done servicing the room," the clerk continues.

Alex tells himself that sinking feeling in his chest isn't disappointment.

Jake gives the clerk a polite smile. "We don't mind coming back."

If we make it, Alex doesn't add. But he declines the clerk's offer to store his bag and makes his way back to the truck.

SO HE AND JAKE SPEND THE AFTERNOON HANGING OUT IN A local coffee shop, not doing much of anything. Or scratch that: Jake spends the afternoon poring over files. Alex spends the afternoon watching Jake.

After a while, Jake looks up from whatever he's reading, touches his fingers to his jaw right at the edge of his stubble, the spot where a dimple appears, sometimes, only when he's truly pleased. That Alex remembers.

"Do I have something on my face?" Jake asks.

Alex could lie. Could say Jake has an invisible spot of coffee, a loose crumb. Now that fake milk is more common, Jake drinks oat milk lattes. His mouth would taste...sweet. "No," Alex says, hoarsely, "nothing on your face."

And gets the flash of a dimple before Jake returns to his reading.

THERE'S NOTHING ALEX HATES MORE IN HORROR MOVIES THAN characters, as they approach an almost certainly haunted house, going *I have a bad feeling about this.*

It's late afternoon. Ghosts don't need full dark to operate —there are plenty of ghosts who clock in at dawn and are happy enough to throw you against the wall at noon. But generally spirits are easier to see in the dark.

As they approach the house—a neatly symmetrical colonial mansion seated near the Hudson, which is also definitely haunted—dread takes root in Alex's belly. He *does* have a bad feeling about this.

At least no one's currently living here: there's a caretaker who comes through a few times a week. Somehow, Jake has his schedule and he's not due for another day. The estate feels neatly abandoned, like its previous inhabitants are long gone and long forgotten. Except for the cry of the wind through the trees. This place *remembers* and every instinct Alex has starts blaring an alarm.

Jake stops on the stone path approaching the house, suddenly enough that Alex nearly runs into his back. He catches Jake by the waist, hands in the safety of his jacket. Once steadied, Alex should pull back. *Should.* But doesn't.

Jake's back tenses as if he's objecting to being held in this way.

"Sorry," Alex breathes. His hands are like the rest of him, stubborn, reluctant to let go.

Especially when Jake says, "Don't be." His eyes slide momentarily shut. He almost, almost leans back against Alex.

Alex remembers, then, the cheap hotel soap smell of his neck. How he'd wake up hard in his bed in Sofia's house and press his face for a second to the cool pillow next to him, seeking that scent, a memory that not even ten years could erase.

"Did you feel that?" Jake asks, low.

For a second, Alex wonders if he's talking about Alex touching him—until Jake casts a look at the woods around them. It's late enough in October that most trees have dropped their leaves. Their bare branches scrape a dour afternoon sky. Ghost-hunting weather.

We could pack it in. They could—could get back in Jake's

truck and retreat to their hotel room. And then what? Ten years ago, Alex would have been the first through the door, the first to crow in victory when they laid a ghost to rest, the first to pull Jake into a creaking motel bed. Now he braces himself as if Jake could suddenly fall and Alex is the only one who could catch him.

His hands still aren't moving. Jake drops a look down at the clasp of them. A strand of his hair almost tickles Alex's nose.

Another wind blows through the forest, bringing voices with it, indistinct, like a conversation from another room. Alex is wearing a sweater under his jacket and a T-shirt under that, and he still comes up in gooseflesh. In front of him, Jake's teeth chatter.

"We don't have to do this," Alex says, but Jake shakes his head.

"We do. They're getting louder." Another click of Jake's teeth. "Soon..." Soon, he'll erode like stone into nothingness. Soon, there won't be anything left of him for Alex to reach out and grasp. Alex eases himself away. But when Jake keeps walking, he follows.

At the door, Jake kneels. For a second, Alex imagines him picking the lock, tools held in the slim confidence of his hands. Instead, he simple retrieves a fake plastic rock from behind a planter and pops it open to reveal a key.

"How'd you know that was there?" Alex asks.

Jake's grins up from where he's still on his knees. "I have my ways." And he laughs at himself. "Mostly, I cased the place for a week."

He starts to get up, and Alex offers his hand, clad in a thick work glove, and is rewarded with the grasp of Jake's palm against his. Alex doesn't know if ten years changed his fascination with Jake's hands—with his long fingers and ridged knuckles and life-roughened palms. Maybe just knowing how much he can't touch Jake makes him want to touch him that much more.

"This time," Alex says, "if you get hurt, I should still use gloves, right?"

Jake swallows visibly; he withdraws his hand from Alex's gloved one. "This time, if I get hurt, you should run."

Run. A decade ago Alex walked away. Now he wouldn't go if someone dragged him. He levels a determined glare at Jake. "I won't leave you behind."

Jake levels a look right back. "There might not be anything to save."

If the world was fair, this would be the moment for Alex to kiss him, for them to press together and shelter each other from the bite of the wind and the voices of the dead. Alex settles for squeezing Jake's fingers gently and watching the light in Jake's eyes and the depths of the dimple on his left cheek and how he breathes. "After..." Jake says, then trails off like he knows they might not survive this but he's hoping that they will.

"I'm not leaving you. Just to be clear."

"Anyone ever tell you that you're stubborn?" Jake grits out.

Alex raises his eyebrows challengingly. "Yes, that is not a trait we share."

The remnants of Jake's smile fade. He eases the key in the lock then slides into the house through the open door, head cocked, listening for alarms. Jake, always careful until he isn't.

After a moment's hesitation, Alex slides him after him.

Inside the house, a haze hangs in the air—dust, possibly. Except every few breaths Alex catches an edge of smoke. His instincts increase their warning. This isn't a place he should be—that *anyone* should be. Perhaps they should have razed the house years ago. Should have cast the family out to haunt the trees and the rocks and the soil. A river flows nearby, far enough to make it an inconvenience to haul water in a fire. Close enough to carry their spirits out to sea.

This isn't our problem, Alex thinks about saying. How much of adulthood is acknowledging when it's not his turn to give a fuck. But of course, that's bullshit, when Jake's holding his shoulders stiff as if he's carrying their memories.

He inspects the front hall, the dust-cloth covered living room, the foodless kitchen, as Alex trails behind. Maybe it's just the memory of having been in the house ten years ago, but Alex smells more and more smoke. His nose itches; his eyes water. Finally, he withdraws a tissue from the pack he stashes in his jacket pocket and dabs at his eyes. It comes away smudged with black like he has on mascara that's begun to run.

"Hey, Jake," he calls, and Jake pauses in his inspection of the uncovered dining room table, "I think they know we're here."

Jake doesn't look up from where he's skimming a hand over the shining waxed surface of the table, as if checking for something.

"Jake," Alex says, more urgently.

Still no response.

It takes four steps for Alex to cross the room. His hands grip Jake's coat. Up close, Jake's eyes have that same pale blue haze they got in the cemetery, when a ghost crawled down his throat and Alex had to preserve him with his own breath. He's digging his fingernails into his palm in desperate semi-circles, one of which is already tinging red.

Worse, something is circulating under his skin like a moving tattoo. Words too faint to make out: an adult's practiced penmanship, a child's less definite chicken-scratched letters. Most devastating of all, an *X* like someone who never learned to sign their own name.

Alex wants to shake him—to shake the ghost out of him or sense into him. "You weren't gonna tell me?" he asks through clenched teeth.

"Just...started..." Jake's speech is slow, slurred like he's not the only voice in his head.

"What do you need?" Alex says. Because he has a bag with a taser in it, a pack of tarot cards that he tossed in on impulse, a body full of instincts screaming at him to get them the fuck out of there.

He thought they'd get more time: that this would be as neat as a séance. Get in, call some spirits down, get out. Not the sudden shock of Jake's possession, the desperation in his voice.

Smoke burns Alex's nostrils—not just the idea of a smell, but a cloud smogging the room. He goes to the curtained windows of the dining room and pushes them back, hoping to cast open a long-shut window and admit fresh air. Behind the curtains, the glass is filmed in soot. Beyond that, thick gray clouds roll through the woods.

He pulls at the window sash. The window does not budge. He presses his palms to the glass and pushes upward. Not a creak. Not the whisper of a breeze from underneath the sill. It's old thick glass, the kind that's heavier toward the bottom of the pane, and Alex should have brought a hammer, but he settles for banging it with his fist to see if the pane will pop out, first cautiously, then in desperation. Nothing.

Behind him, Jake coughs like he's drowning in smoke.

Alex wrenches the taser from his bag, activates it, and

flicks it through the smoke like ineffective lightning. Faintly, a noise crackles like a ghost of a laugh.

"Stop it," Alex shouts to the ghosts around them. "Cut it the fuck out."

This time the laugh is closer to his ear, a high childish giggle that goes feral at the end, like the ghosts have loosed whatever fraying stitches kept them human. A laugh, then a whisper like paper, a smell like old smoke, a sensation of ice crawling across his skin. Blackness starts to encroach on his vision.

"Jake," he scrapes out. His throat is tight, closing like anaphylaxis. Alex has CPR training and Narcan training and EpiPen training, and he wishes for something as simple as plunging a long needle into his thigh. *I thought we'd get more time. I thought they would have forgotten us.* As if time matters to the unburied dead.

Jake's on him, hands at Alex's jacket, loosening it, then his sweater and shirt. "Breathe," he orders, and Alex takes in a staggering gasp of air. "Good. Again."

He does, a breath, another, and he focuses enough to realizes two things: he's breathing a little easier and Jake's palms are under his shirt against the bare skin of his chest.

"What are you doing?" Alex coughs.

"It's fine." Which isn't an answer—isn't even approaching an answer. Except for the faint mist bridging the distance between them, as if Jake is drawing out the ghost like poison from a wound. His eyes are glowing blue now, a color that extends to his lips and the thin skin at his temples.

Alex tries to pull away. "Stop."

"Let me do this."

Soot starts to snow down from somewhere in the ceiling,

enough to speckle Jake's hair, to dot his cheeks like a parody of his freckles.

"I won't let you do this." Alex catches Jake's wrists and tugs and finally, finally, Jake pulls his hands away.

Instantly, Alex's throat tightens again, and he takes another gasp like sucking a too-thick milkshake through a straw. He wheezes, then rasps, then can't even get that noise out.

"I'm sorry," Jake says.

Alex shakes his head, trying to tell him that he chose this. That if he goes out like this, at least they're together.

"I'm sorry," Jake says, again. He grabs Alex by his shirt and presses a glance of a kiss to his cheek. His lips are cold.

I won't get to say goodbye. And then Alex is plunged into darkness.

ALEX COMES TO LIKE BEING DROPPED BACK INTO HIS BODY from a great height. He's on the floor and Jake's lying beside him, shoulder to shoulder, the way they did in the cemetery grass. This close, Jake smells like smoke, like coffee and cheap soap. There's blood at his hairline. More is caked at his ear. He's examining his own wrist, watching dark lines creep their way up it like rot, like tendrils of ink.

He's dying, Alex realizes. "You shouldn't have done that."

Jake glances over. The ends of his hair brush Alex's face. It's strange to mourn for something he won't get again, but that's what Alex does, a clench in his gut that says *This is it.* "Done what?" Asked like he doesn't know. He must. This whole situation must be painfully obvious: they charged in underprepared, overwhelmed. This entire thing was doomed right from the start.

"Saved me like that."

"Hmmm…" A *Jake* disagreement that makes Alex want to throttle him. "Sorry."

"You don't sound sorry."

Jake's laugh rattles his chest. "That's cause I'm not."

"You shouldn't give your life up that easily."

"Don't take this the wrong way, but nothing about you is easy." Jake coughs hoarsely like there's something lodged in his throat. Ten years, a cemetery's worth of ghosts. "If I had to do this over, I'd probably prefer not to end up dead, but what can you do?"

If I had to do this over… Would he have followed Jake to that cemetery? The thing is, Alex might. No, Alex *would*.

"It's probably silly," Jake continues, "but when I thought about death, I always imagined being reabsorbed back into space. Like one second you're alive and the next you're back to being star stuff." Tears trace their way through the soot on his cheeks. This version of his smile is the worst one: fond, with a sort of peaceful resignation. "Whatever patch of universe I end up as, I always wanted it to be right next to yours."

Alex can't breathe. From the smoke, from the ghost threading its way out of his lungs. From the sensation sitting on his chest, a heavy weight of regret that they wasted so much fucking *time*.

"No," he gasps, and Jake looks over at him in surprise, "we're not saying goodbye." He strips the glove from his hand, then catches Jake at his wrist, thumb and index finger on the thin drumbeat of Jake's pulse. "If we're doing this, we're doing it together."

Jake is shaking his head. "One of us should make it. One of should live."

"We're dying—but we're not dead yet." Alex coughs

around another mouthful of smoke. "Now trust me. I have a good feeling about this."

Jake's laugh is a phantom of its normal self. "You sure about this?" he asks.

His wrist is cool under Alex's fingers. Mist keeps hopping between them as if the ghosts aren't sure where to settle. Alex remembers this feeling: this bull-headed certainty. And that's enough to make him sit up, body propped on his elbows, fingers adamant on Jake's wrist.

Above them, ghosts swirl in an angry cloud. *What do you want?* Alex almost asks. What everyone asks of ghosts. *Tell us how to fix this and we'll send you on your way.* How lonely they must be, trapped here, doomed to relieve the worst night of their lives. How lonely Jake must have been to carry their memories by himself.

Anger fills Alex's belly—familiar and clarifying. "The world's different now," Alex calls up. "It's moved on from when you died."

"Seriously?" Jake hisses.

Alex heaves a one-shouldered shrug. Even that aches. His chest and stomach feel like they've been hollowed out and put back together wrong. "Thought I'd try something else."

"Only you would try pissing them off." And if Alex didn't know better, he'd think Jake's voice caught on *only you.* Then Jake smiles—that smile he'd get when Alex talked him into something. "Yeah," he shouts, "world's different now. We got all kinds of stuff. Gay marriage. Baseball cards. Waffles—I bet you've never had waffles. And um, fuck, what's some other stuff?"

Alex laughs. "Stop making me laugh when my lungs hurt."

Which makes Jake laugh. "I could say the same thing."

Above them the fog really has stopped moving. If mist could look inquisitive, this one does.

"There's so much out in the world," Jake says, finally. "Too much sometimes. It can be overwhelming." His voice goes thick. "Some days, you can't do anything but go out into it: it's noisy and messy and so, so lonely that you don't know what to do. But you should see it for yourself while you can."

The fog whispers a question. *How?*

Jake shrugs. "You kind of have to make it up as you go. That's the secret. That's what we're all doing, even when we're pretending we have it all figured out. Sometimes you make bad decisions, ones you have to carry with you. Ones you end up regretting and aren't sure you know how to fix." He turns to Alex, eyelashes a brush against his cheek. "And sometimes you meet someone who gives you another chance. Who sees you for however messed up you are and for whatever reason, says, *yeah, that one*. That's the stuff that doesn't fade." He swallows. Turns back to the ceiling. "So go. But bring each other. It's better when you're with someone you love."

In the smoke, his eyes are green and gray and laughing, and Alex wants to kiss him but settles for reaching for Jake's hand, clasping it in his own. Memories come with it, flashing like cards from a spilled deck, too fast for Alex to register one fully before the next overtakes it. Some carry images, some only fast blinks of light. Smoke fills Alex's mouth, his lungs, his mind, until he feels like he's made of nothing else, like he and Jake are floating in a universe of two.

For a second, a stillness echoes through the house. Then flame—bright, blinding—pours out from the doorway and the pops out each pane from the windows.

And just as suddenly as it began, it ends, leaving only a drift of dust motes and the lingering smell of something long-burned.

Jake's hand is still clasped in his. Jake withdraws it slowly, like he's in no hurry, a brush of their palms together that makes Alex greedy for more. He sits up, slow, woozy, and Alex reaches out an arm to support him, and gets the effort of Jake's cough.

"They're gone?" Alex asks, low, in case the ghosts change their minds.

"They're gone," Jake confirms. His face is damp—sweat? No, he wipes his hand under his eyes, flicking away tears.

"Here." Alex digs in his pocket for that plastic pack of tissues, holding it out.

Jake takes the Kleenex, blotting his face with it. "It's probably stupid to mourn people who tried to kill us a bunch."

"You wouldn't be you if you didn't." That same urge to kiss him hasn't gone anywhere, but Alex offers his hand.

For a second, he wonders if Jake's fingers will slide through his, like combing through mist. That they'll have failed and be stuck here like the family before them. Alex can imagine worse fates than spending an eternity watching the slow crease of Jake's smile and hearing the delight of his laughter.

"We shouldn't..." Jake looks at his hand like he doesn't know what to do. "It's not safe for us to touch, probably. Not while their memories are fresh."

So Alex slides his glove back on and gets the reassuring grasp of Jake's hand in his. Then he leads them out into the clear afternoon light.

6

———

THEY STUMBLE THEIR WAY BACK TO JAKE'S TRUCK, THROUGH A short drive—Jake's face pressed against the window, and Alex would think he was asleep if not for his smile as Alex fumbled for the levers to move his seat forward. Jake drags himself through the hotel lobby, leans heavy against the mirrored wall of the elevator as Alex studies the infinity of his reflection.

They collapse out of the elevator, up the short hallway to their room. The door has barely closed before Jake begins a slow collapse toward the carpet. His face is still streaked with soot. He coughs, once, weakly. *At least he's still breathing.* Even if those breaths are thready and shallow.

Alex wants to—he doesn't know. Kiss him to prove they're both alive. That the world around them is still alive. Because it's barely dinnertime on a Thursday and they *survived.*

He does none of that. Instead he seizes Jake by his shirtsleeve, careful not to touch his skin even incidentally, and pulls him toward the bathroom. "You should clean up," Alex says more gruffly than he means to, but it puts some vigor back into Jake's spine and he lets himself be led.

The stall is one of those confusing ones with a frosted glass panel as an excuse for a curtain. Jake stares at it like he doesn't know what's happening. His fingers trace numbly over the zipper on his vest.

"I got it," Alex breathes, then pulls the zipper down, the click of its teeth loud in the otherwise quiet bathroom, and lets Jake shrug the vest off.

Jake pulls off his own T-shirt, the collar smudging the streaks on his face, then stalls out, looking down helplessly at his laced-up sneakers. Alex forgot what this was like— Jake, *after*, his body a repository for ghosts. No, forgetting would imply he simply discarded the memory. This he didn't want to remember, not the ashen tint to Jake's skin, the subtle shake in his hands like he's too worn down to undress himself.

Alex kneels, undoes one lace, then the next, then offers his shoulder as Jake steps out of his shoes. Shirtless, in his socked feet, Jake looks even more vulnerable, adrift on the bathroom tile, and Alex tamps down the part of himself that wants to pull Jake into his arms and to draw a wet washrag over his face. To touch him and tell him that things will be okay.

Jake's already pushing down his pants, which fall in a thump onto the bathroom floor. He tugs off each sock, then pauses as if waiting for Alex to vacate the bathroom. "I'm gonna shower."

"Yeah," Alex says, because he can take a hint.

"Could you, uh..." Jake trails off. His eyes are glassy, bordering on unfocused, and maybe Alex should get him some orange juice. *Or therapy.*

"...wait in here?" Jake finishes.

It takes a second to put the sentence together. "Sure." Alex eyes that half-open shower stall. There's no way to sit here and not see Jake. Perhaps whatever remained of their modesty with one another got burned up in the fire.

Either way, Jake pads into the shower stall and strips his boxers off, tossing them out onto the pile of his clothes. He turns the water on, and the bathroom is small enough and the hotel water heater capacious enough that the mirror begins to fog immediately.

Alex leans against the counter and attempts to scroll through his phone, though his eyes drift over to the lean line of Jake's body behind the frosted glass panel.

Especially when Jake gives a long-relieved sigh. "Could you pass me the shampoo?" Alex does, along with a washcloth at Jake's request, and watches his shadowed outline as he begins with his face and works his way, finally bending to scrub his ankles and feet.

He's fine. You can leave. But Alex sits, transfixed. There's something casually intimate about hearing the squish and scrape of a hotel washcloth across Jake's skin and his groans of relief as he cleans himself off. Something Alex missed, along with Jake occupying the other half his bed and stealing food off his plate and all the things he didn't even know he was missing. For ten years.

A few minutes later—soon, too soon—Jake cuts the water off. Alex picks up a towel from the neat hotel-folded stack of them and holds it out. Jake grabs it, and Alex should let him get dried off, should leave, should go contemplate what his life will be like after this when Jake says, "I can still hear them."

That makes Alex stop. "I thought they were gone."

Jake emerges, a towel wound around his waist, though it's too short to make it all the way, so he clutches it with one hand. And Alex won't leer at the triangle of thigh he flashes or the flat cut of muscle low on his belly—or the necklace sitting in the hollow of his throat like Jake didn't want to take off something Alex bought for him.

"They are gone," Jake says. "I can just hear them. It's hard to explain. It's like...you know when you go to bed and then you lie there and turn something over and over again in your mind when you're supposed to be sleeping?"

Not really. "Sure."

Jake laughs. The towel slips minutely, and Alex should get out of this steamy little bathroom, where Jake's hair is still clinging to the nape of his neck, and his body carries all the scars of their ten years apart that Alex wants to spend the next ten years finding out about. And they can't.

"Well, it's like that." Jake shrugs. "It's fine."

It's fine. What Jake always said ten years ago, and Alex believed him, because believing him was easier. "It's okay if it's not."

Jake's eyebrows rise in question.

"Not fine," Alex clarifies. "You could tell me."

Jake gives him an indecipherable look, and his eyes aren't grayer or greener, but there's a shine to them that maybe wasn't there before. Slowly, he nods. "I'll probably be able to sleep." At that, he pads into the other room, dropping the towel, and pulling on a pair of boxers. He doesn't bother with any clothing beyond that, just slides into the bed closer to the door like he's trying to prove a point to Alex or himself or the ghosts.

Alex spends the next few minutes cleaning himself up. He goes out into the hall long enough to buy two bottles of water from the vending machine then, with some hesitation, a pack of those peanut butter crackers that Jake used to eat by the handful.

When he gets back into the room, Jake's eyes are shut, but his breathing is uneven like he's staving something off. Alex sets the water and crackers on the nightstand.

"Thanks," Jake croaks out.

It should not affect Alex. Alex should strip off his own clothes and climb into the other bed. Alex should not make the same mistakes he did when he was twenty-three. In the interim, he's gotten a master's degree, a decent credit score, and opinions about how credit scores are mostly bullshit: he's grown up. They've grown apart. The last time this happened, he watched Jake do this again and again until finally he had to walk away.

Every sane, mature part of him says to walk across the room, turn the lights off, and go the fuck to sleep.

Instead he sits on the edge of the bed, insulated from Jake's body by a cushy white hotel comforter. "Hey," he whispers, low, like he might disturb the ghosts rippling beneath Jake's skin.

Jake stirs against his pillow, slitting open an eye. "Hey." Said equally low.

"Can't sleep?"

Jake shakes his head and doesn't bother to deny that he was pretending—and some decade-old part of Alex clenches at Jake pretending *for him.*

"What helps?" Alex asks.

For that, he gets a shrug of Jake's shoulder under the comforter. "You brought me peanut butter crackers?"

"Yeah."

"Then that helps."

"I could get you donuts," Alex offers.

Jake smiles, a smile that's more tired than sleepy. "Stay. Please."

Alex reaches a hand out and, with some hesitance,

traces his fingers through the ends of Jake's hair. It's soft and still slightly damp, drying in waves. Jake's breath goes short, like he's waiting for disaster to strike.

Maybe Alex shouldn't. Maybe every part of Jake down to the fingernails acts as a transmitter and Alex will be plunged into the same misery of hearing an echo of ghosts when he shuts his eyes.

Jake's hair is soft under his fingers. The lines by Jake's eyes relax but don't entirely fade. No strange haze falls over Alex's vision, no blur of other people's memories. "You could tell me about them," Alex says.

"About who?"

"The ghosts. Any of them."

Jake blinks both his eyes open. "Like a story? Most people are pretty boring."

"So tell me a boring story."

Jake doesn't say anything for a second. Alex hasn't withdrawn his hand from his hair. He should. Except he doesn't want to. Except that feeling, the one he thought he left ten years in the past, is back. That he can look nowhere but Jake's face, can focus on no sound but his breathing, and the gentle cut of his smile. "Okay," Jake says, "but you have to write it down."

Alex doesn't argue. He gets the hotel-branded notepad and pen from the dresser, then sits back down on the bed. Through the comforter, Jake huddles closer, hip against the line of Alex's thigh. His eyes are closed again; his breathing more even. It's possible he will actually just fall asleep. Alex should want that: Jake, with some peace. Jake, who saved his life, who carries ghosts under his skin.

Who Alex still cares about after ten years, despite his best efforts not to.

"I thought of something," Jake murmurs.

Alex readies his pen, tip poised over a fresh notepad sheet.

"William—the younger son—liked to wave to the birds in their nests on his way to school. Once he was late because he got distracted looking at the shape of tree branches against the sky." Jake hums at that, as if he's relieving the memory, as if he's feeling a dirt path beneath the hard sole of a child-sized shoe. "He liked to be outside. The teachers were always rapping his knuckles about it. He'd stare out the window and wish he was out playing in a creek or running. His parents should have been mad about it, but they never were."

And Alex writes that all down, pen scratching as it passes over the rough surface of the paper. "Which creek?" he asks.

Jake's smile expands. "The one that used to run near his house. It's not there anymore. Gentrification, I guess."

Alex laughs. "Yeah, probably. What else?"

"How long would you do this for?" As if he's imposing on Alex's time.

I thought I'd forgotten what it was like to be with you. Even if the memory never faded entirely—just hid someplace below Alex's consciousness for safekeeping. "Is it helping?"

Jake nods.

"Then as long as you want."

This time, Jake's smile is something electric. "Okay." And he keeps talking.

An hour later, Alex's hand is cramping around the pen. Jake's words slur slightly at the edges with sleep. He's blinking like he's making an effort to keep his eyes open.

"You should rest," Alex says. All the lights are off—he dimmed them halfway into this—except the bedside lamp that lights up the reddish parts of Jake's hair.

Jake nods and snuggles into the blanket. "It's quieter in here."

The sound level in the room hasn't changed much, save the noise from passing cars. Still, it feels quieter, with Jake's soft breathing. With the faint shush of the heating system blowing warm air. With the ghosts clattering around Jake's mind safely stored on paper. Alex should sleep too. He puts the pad down on the bedside table, then stands. His knees crack from having been sitting for so long. He glances over in case he's managed to rouse Jake.

"You going to bed?" Jake breathes.

"Yeah." Even if the other bed feels like it's both five feet and a mile away.

Jake pats the blanket covering him. "Technically, this is a bed."

A sentence that makes Alex pause. The hotel is nice: two queen-sized beds that are actually queen-sized and not the full-sized ones cheaper places pretend are larger. From what Alex remembers, Jake likes to sleep close.

"I thought..." Alex begins. *I thought your skin was lit up with ghosts.* "I thought we couldn't touch."

Jake rolls and sits up. The comforter drapes down to his waist, showing off the lean line of his torso. Alex would call it dirty pool if he objected. At all.

Jake catches him looking—an easy feat because Alex is done pretending he isn't—and waves a hand to indicate his own scar-covered skin. "It's better now," Jake says. "Less noisy." What he said before—that it was quieter. Not in the room, but inside himself.

"You sure?" Alex is struck by the same image he got that

first time Jake invaded his library and his personal space: of the curl of Jake's hand in the spikes of his hair. A fantasy, he thought at the time. But that was a memory. How could whatever they do now possibly hold up to ten years ago? Alex almost talks himself out of it. Almost tells Jake that he should really get some sleep when Jake lowers the blanket another inch. "Maybe we should test that out," Alex says instead.

Jake smiles. This one Alex classifies as mischievous. *Flirtatious*, even. "Try it."

Alex could simply apply his palm to Jake's forehead as if checking for a fever or catch his fingers and thumb around the circle of Jake's wrist. There are an infinite number of ways for two people to touch. Right now, the catalog of them sends heat across Alex's skin.

So he places the pad of his index finger on the lines by Jake's eyes and waits for memories to bridge the connection, to jump from Jake's body to his. Instead, there's only the softness of the skin there, the blink of Jake's eyelashes. The slow turn of his cheek until his lips brush Alex's palm.

"See," Jake says, "it's safe."

No part about this feels safe, most especially not the kiss Jake applies to the heel of his hand. Not the way Alex cups his face and tilts up his chin, then presses his mouth to Jake's, long and tasting and slow.

Jake kisses the way Alex remembers and like something entirely new. Alex wants to drink the stories off his tongue, the ones that made him kiss different than he did a decade ago, the ones that made him wind his arms around Alex as if no time has passed at all.

Slowly, Alex lowers himself in increments. They might not fit together as they once did—Alex doesn't know if he can take the realization that they've grown apart, literally. That certain things once lost are unrecoverable.

"C'mon," Jake says and tightens his arms.

Alex does, finally, settling his thighs on either side of Jake's hips, and kissing the ridge of his collarbone and the long line of his neck, fingers drifting over the steady rhythm of his heart.

"Do you remember…" Jake says, and Alex braces himself for nostalgia, for Jake longing for the version of himself that's ten years gone, "…me sitting outside the library for a week before I finally worked up the nerve to come in?"

Alex pulls back to look at him in question. "No?"

Jake doesn't flush, but he bites his lip like he's pleasantly embarrassed. "I just wanted to see you. It'd been so long. You seemed so happy." Jake's embarrassment shifts toward shame. "I didn't want to bring you back into this if I could help it. I was hoping you'd just think I was some guy with a weird hobby."

"You're not?" Alex teases.

"This isn't me trying to drag you away again," Jake adds. "This doesn't have to *be* anything."

Now Alex pulls back, blinking down at him. "Jake, you saved my life."

"That doesn't make this an obligation or whatever." He shrugs, as if it's not a big deal. "I spend half my time worrying I'll accidentally touch someone. It makes it easier…not to."

Alex soothes a hand down his chest to his belly, skimming over the line of hair that descends from his navel. He follows it to Jake's waistband, then upward, determined to memorize every scar and bump, relishing the slight shake of Jake's muscles and the hesitant intake of his breath.

"When was the last time someone touched you like this?" Alex asks.

"I don't think anyone's ever touched me the way you touch me." Jake says it all in a rush, like the admission was pulled from somewhere deep within him.

"How long do we have?"

Jake glances over at the green-lettered alarm clock. "Um, I think checkout's at ten."

Alex laughs and lowers himself down again, chest to Jake's, hands winding their way in his hair.

Whatever hesitancies Alex had that they wouldn't slot together are now replaced by fears that they'll have to pull apart. "I meant," Alex whispers, "how long before I can't touch you again."

"Oh." Jake glances at the clock again. "Probably not until morning."

So Alex kisses him, deep and unwavering. "Then I guess we'll just have to make the most of it."

Jake smiles back into the kiss. Of all the ways he smiles, this is Alex's favorite: a smile that's punctuated by the bite of his teeth, the roughness of his palms as he traces his way over Alex's body. Alex works hard to not become soft-handed. He lifts weights and does carpentry and plays guitar and digs in Sofia's garden on a padded kneeling mat that's his concession to getting older. But he can't deny that some of his life is now spent typing and frowning at spreadsheets and on endless Zoom calls.

Jake's calluses scratch across his skin, down Alex's ribs, around the softened curve of his belly.

"Desk job," Alex says. He means it halfway to an apology because he spent his twenties thinking of himself as stocky and his thirties actually being stocky, and he doesn't know how his current self squares with Jake's memory of him.

Jake frowns minutely, then seizes his hand, winding their fingers together. Closes his eyes. Tension radiates in the lines around his eyes. He pinches his tongue against his teeth in concentration, something Alex has only about half a second to find cute when a vision like a second monitor drops over his vision.

The hair on his arm stands up. A faint thunderish crackle fills the room. Alex is met by something he doesn't quite know is happening until it is—a memory from Jake's perspective, Alex in his full library drag, lifting the ghost-hunting equipment off the lower shelf. Jake's appraisal of the thickness of his back and thighs, the hope his shirt would ride up to reveal a sliver of skin, the disappointment when it didn't.

"Really?" Alex says, both to the realization that Jake can apparently send memories his way and that Jake decided to do that with a memory of him ogling Alex's ass.

Jake releases their hands then cycles through a few rounds of breathing like that kind of control took effort. "When I said you look good, I meant you looked *good*." And he tilts his head up like he's demanding a kiss—so Alex obliges him.

That kiss turns to another, turns to Jake's long groan into his mouth when Alex rolls his hips and scrapes his teeth on Jake's neck, then sucks a purple mark there for good measure, big and mouth-shaped and obvious. Something that Jake'll wear out of here tomorrow, going out into the world carrying Alex on his skin.

"If you're gonna do that—" Jake begins and Alex expects a mid-thirties objection to being given a hickey, before Jake continues, "make me feel it." He stretches, long and lean, hands braced against the half-moon of the hotel headboard, emphasizing the purple traffic of veins at his wrists.

Jake told him nothing about him was easy, but Alex *feels* easy this way. Easy in the way he seizes Jake's wrists, easy in the way he bears his weight down on Jake. "More," Jake grunts, like he can't get enough of Alex, and Alex lowers his entire body onto his and gets the compliment of Jake's moan.

The blanket is still bunched between them and Alex peels himself off long enough to drag it down and onto the floor.

"Good thing this place comes with two beds," Jake says.

Alex pauses in his arrangement of the comforter. "How's that?"

"Fuck in one and sleep in the other." What they never bothered with, before—not when Alex could have pretty much screwed and slept on any flat surface and some not so flat ones.

"There are some advantages to not being twenty-three," Alex concedes.

Jake sends a hand down below his own waistband to where his cock is visibly thickening in his boxers. "Maybe." Then he frowns. Those lines of tension are back by his eyes, the version of them that Alex wants to immediately chase away. "I'm on some medications," Jake says. "They can make me take a long time to come."

That's also new. Ten years ago, sex was like the rest of their lives together: fast and rough. Alex glances over at the clock, ticking down until Jake's skin will no longer be safe to touch. "We have until tomorrow?" Alex confirms.

Jake nods.

"I guess I'll let you come before then."

And Jake's eyes go briefly wide. He laughs, heels digging in the mattress. "Oh, you'll *let* me?"

"I might not." Alex means it as a threat but something in Jake's face goes equally shocked and pleased.

"What if I ask *really* nicely?" Jake asks.

So Alex makes a brief detour over to his bag, out of which he retrieves a bottle of lube that he tosses on the bed.

Jake examines it, turning it over like he's reading the ingredients. "There's vegan lube?" he asks, incredulous.

"I was surprised you remembered about the vegan thing," Alex says. "I gave it up a while ago anyway."

"I remember everything." For a moment, Jake sounds regretful—that he carries memories whether he wants them or not. Then a faint flush creeps over his cheeks. "But I especially remember when it comes to you."

"Fuck, Alex, I'm about to…" Jake says, for the third time in an hour.

Alex eases his hand off him before he can come. His lubed palm leaves a smear across the bedsheet. Good thing the room came with two beds. "Thought you said this was going to take a while."

Jake cracks an eye open. He's flushed and splotchy to his chest, cock leaking as Alex draws the tip of his finger over it, then reaches to cup his balls. He squeezes gently enough that Jake groans. He's kicked the sheets all over—the top one is lolling over one side of the bed. Even the fitted one has started to come loose and Alex is only somewhat smug about that.

He's equally smug when Jake whines, high up in his throat, as Alex presses two fingers behind his balls. Desk worker hands might be soft, but Jake doesn't seem to mind writhing against his knuckles. Or hasn't minded the last three times Alex has done this before he pulls back entirely to watch Jake squirm.

In the last hour, he's discovered Jake likes when Alex sits across his thighs, likes when he leaves toothmarks on his chest, likes when Alex wrings his cock with enough pressure that he must be in slight pain then follows it with the loose circle of his fist. Likes all those enough that his eyes are slightly wet at the eyelashes.

"Too much?" Alex asks while Jake regains his breath.

Jake smirks. "Almost enough."

Alex can't remember if they talked this much in bed a decade ago or if they approached sex with the same bravado they approached everything else, but all he can think is *new memories* as he pours more lube on his hand, as he listens to Jake's pleas for Alex to finally, finally give him what he wants.

7

———

When Alex wakes up the next morning, Jake is already awake and dressed and sitting on the other bed. "Checkout's actually at eleven," he says. "I brought you some breakfast."

Which he did: a cup of coffee and another of orange juice, a bagel with packets of butter and jam sitting next to it, and Jake said this didn't have to be *anything*, but Alex isn't sure how it isn't. Especially not when Jake grins down at him, the Jake *morning after* smile Alex somehow, impossibly, blotted out for ten years.

Alex sits up, letting the sheet fall down to his waist. Jake's eyes fall with it, over the plains of Alex's chest and the rise of his stomach, and Alex would be vaguely apologetic for not being twenty-three again if he didn't spend last night wringing noises of pleasure from the back of Jake's throat.

Even with creamer, the coffee tastes burned, and Alex frowns at it and gets Jake's laugh. "We'll get something better on the road," Jake promises.

The road. *Home.* Where Alex has a day job and a set of books and a bed in Sofia's house and a life. Jake called him happy, and he is, in the small ways that he's come to realize constitute happiness: steadiness and community and purpose.

Take me with you on the next trip, Alex doesn't say. Because he doesn't want to go, not really, but he doesn't want to say goodbye. Instead he takes another sip of terrible coffee that nevertheless puts warmth in his belly.

With anyone else—a date, a one-night stand—Alex would pull them back into bed. There's an hour before they have to be out of the room. They could use it. But Jake's already in a pair of joggers and hoodie, his hands settled in its front pocket.

"Are you cold?" Alex asks. At Jake's look of confusion, he nods to his hands.

Jake shakes his head. "I got a little longer than normal, but I probably shouldn't touch you." He flexes his hands in the pocket of his sweatshirt for emphasis.

Alex shouldn't like that Jake needs a tactile reminder to keep his hands off him, but he does. "Yeah."

"It fucking sucks, I know." Jake's smile goes tight. "I think you writing all that stuff down helped. Ghosts don't like competing stories."

Alex turned to the notepad still on the dresser. "We could bring it with us. Write more in the car."

"You'll probably get tired of it at some point." Though *tired of it* sounds a lot like *tired of me*.

"I'm a librarian," Alex says. "Stories are kind of the whole deal."

Jake's smile softens at the edges. "I guess that's true."

"Let me drink this"—and Alex chugs half the coffee in one gulp, even as his stomach lining objects—"and get cleaned up." But he doesn't jump out of bed. Just reaches for Jake's hand, still ensconced in his hoodie, and strokes his fingers across the fabric'd ridge of Jake's knuckles. "This okay?"

"Yeah." Jake's voice is hoarse, and Alex remembers the shape of it around his name—how Jake panted beneath him. "It's been a long time since I've really been with anyone. Ten years, give or take."

And Alex wants to take him into his arms again and press his face to the back of Jake's neck, and fall asleep with Jake no farther than the other side of the bed, but he settles for stroking his fingers again, separated by fabric, then gets up to throw himself in the shower.

JAKE TALKS FOR MOST OF THE TIME ON THE ROAD, GHOST stories that bridge into stories from the past decade, some well-worn, some ones he doesn't tell many other people from the way the tops of his cheekbones go vaguely pink.

I missed you, Alex thinks. *I missed this.* And he spends the next story divided between listening and considering about what'll happen when they get back to Providence and Alex has to go back to his real life.

"—anyway," Jake is saying, "I told them not to cut my shirt off me, but they didn't listen. The guy ended up puking for an hour."

Alex glances over in slight horror. "That bad?"

"All the stuff with my"—Jake gestures to himself, then immediately returns his hand to the wheel—"got worse pretty soon after you left."

Alex swallows a sip of his better than hotel, but not actually good, coffee along with a dose of guilt. "Yeah."

"It's not because of you," Jake says. "There aren't a lot of doctors who treat ghost possession side effects, but they were all pretty sure this is just how I am."

"Yeah?"

He gets Jake's grin, an easier one than he had on in the hotel room. "Shit just kinda happens, I guess."

Alex can't help but smile back. "I guess it does."

They pull into Providence mid-day, Jake parking in front of Sofia's house.

"How much longer are you in town for?" Alex asks, because Jake mentioned his lease was month-to-month.

Even with the truck parked, Jake's hands are tense on the wheel. "Not sure."

"You have time to come in?"

A smile plays at the edge of Jake's mouth. "I could make the time."

Inside, the house is as Alex left it: artistic, cluttered. *Home.* He gestures to things as they pass them—Sofia's tarot reading setup, her wife's drums, his cousin's artwork. It'd probably be easier to have the conversation he wants to have at the kitchen table, but instead he finds himself leading Jake up to his room.

The bed takes up most of the space—it's large enough that when Alex sits at one end and Jake, with some hesitation, sits at the other, they don't touch.

"I was thinking," Alex says, "I've never built a bed before. I could put another one in here if you ever want a place to stay."

Jake turns to him in surprise.

"And," Alex continues, "the historical society is always looking for people who know local history. Ghosts are local."

"Alex..."

"I don't want you to stop hunting, if that's what you

want," Alex says. "But I was thinking, maybe it'd be okay if you had a place to come back to. If you wanted that."

"Is this really..." Jake begins then recalibrates. "My skin gives people ghost contact highs—or you know what I mean."

Alex affects a shrug. "No one's perfect."

Jake laughs at that, big and loud, then settles. "You deserve someone who you can touch. Who can touch you."

"There's more than one way to be with someone—"

Jake's shaking his head now, like he's building his way toward an argument, less like one he's having with Alex and more like one he's having with himself. "You'll say that but then it's gonna sink in that we can't just touch whenever we want, and it'll be all fine for a while until it isn't and—"

"Jake"—Alex wrenches open the bedside drawer displaying a not insignificant number of sex toys, including some that operate remotely through an app on his phone— "there's more than one way to be with someone."

Jake turns a particular shade of pink. "Oh." He considers the open drawer. "You really thought about this?"

Alex nods. "If it doesn't work, we'll figure out something that will."

This version of Jake's smile Alex remembers: nervous, hopeful, with a glint like he wants to take on the world. He slides his hand under the quilt and after a second, Alex places his own on top of it, feeling Jake's warmth through the layers of fabric.

"It might not work," Jake says, "but I want to try."

Alex tightens his hand across Jake's. "I do too."

EPILOGUE
THREE MONTHS LATER

"Sorry," Alex says not for the first time. He's got one end of a bed frame and Jake has the other, and he measured everything three, four, five times, but didn't account for the bend in the staircase leading up to his room. *Their room.* Or what will be their room once they drop off this bed.

Building a bed took longer than Alex hoped. Especially when Jake took to hanging out in the woodshop with him, bundled in a coat and complaining of the wind when Alex left the garage door open for ventilation.

Especially when Alex distracted himself by touching Jake through the thick padding of his jacket. It was working. They were making it work.

Except for now, given the rigidity of the bedframe and old house stairs.

"I could disassemble it," Alex offers. Though that would mean going at the bedframe with a mallet and possibly ruining all the careful joins he made.

"No." Jake turns, angling the bed this way and that, then grunts in frustration. "We are getting this thing upstairs."

"You're stubborn," Alex says fondly.

Jake gives him a veiled look. "Yes, that is not a trait we share."

Alex adjusts the bedframe again. "If we just…" He turns it once more, and something in that angle does it—the frame and posts clear the impediment of the banister. "Let's go," he says, "before this thing changes its mind."

Jake goes, backing himself up the stairs as Alex follows, and they manage to slide the frame through the high doorway and into the bedroom with ease. Once inside, they turn it horizontally and set it down with a thump.

Alex uses the hem of his shirt to wipe his own sweating face and when he looks up, Jake is standing beside the frame, eying it warily.

"Are you sure Sofia doesn't mind me moving in?" Jake asks, as if there's another question buried under it.

"She doesn't."

"Are you sure?"

"C'mere."

Jake does, accepting Alex's hands on his shoulders. This close, ghosts hum under his skin, the whispers that used to keep them both up at night now circulating like white noise. In recent months, the sounds have gotten quieter, like the swirl of ghosts has settled.

Now Alex can practically taste the crackle of static emanating off him.

"If Sofia didn't like you," Alex says, "she'd turn you into a newt."

Jake laughs. "Funny. She can't do that."

"Don't be so sure." Alex adjusts his hands, tracing a finger over one of the seams, applying pressure to the cords of muscle in his upper back. There are an infinite number of ways for two people to touch—Alex wants his every infinity so long as Jake wants it too. "You still want to do this?"

Jake bites his lip. "I do."

"Then be here."

Jake's smile creases the corners of his eyes, and Alex pulls him close, hands a sweep up his back. "There's one more thing," Alex says, pulling back. "Wait here."

He descends the stairs two at a time, then retrieves an object from the woodshop that he tucked away in a box. This one is easier to carry, even with the same stressed patter to his heart: the hope that Jake will like it. That Jake will get what he's trying to say.

When he gets back upstairs, Jake looks up from his notebook—he's been writing everything down more, snatches of ghosts' stories, long-forgotten memories that he's been holding for safekeeping. Each one helps. Each one unwinds the tension from his shoulders, calms the buzz under his skin, even as he goes out into the world to collect more.

On days when he does nothing more than sit at the library to write, Alex spends more time than he should just looking at him, like if he doesn't, Jake might disappear in a slant of sunlight.

A few of the library kids have noticed—they call him "Mr. Jake" and demand he tells them some of his tamer stories. And sometimes Alex sits on the rug and watches Jake talk and the kids listen and Alex thinks *We could do this. We could have this.*

If *this* is beds that they can move apart and then together, and a schedule that says *hunting* and *writing*, and lists Alex's shifts. He got invited back to Thursday night poker and he loses just enough to have a good time. Small things that accumulate and accumulate and, eventually, start to add up to a life.

All of which he wants to hand to Jake, but he settles for

holding a box nervously and watching as Jake scribbles things down, as he combs his fingers through his hair.

Eventually, Jake looks up at him and smiles, then nods to the box. "What's that?"

"I made you something."

"You made me a whole bed."

"Yes, and something else."

"You didn't have to."

"I wanted to." Words sometimes get stuck somewhere between Alex's chest and throat, but these come easy. "I want to make you things. For a while. If you want that too."

It's not quite a question, but Jake must hear it anyway. "I was thinking I might crochet a couple blankets for the bed."

"Yeah?" Alex asks. "Those could take a while."

That gets Jake's smile. "I'm kind of hoping they will."

"Here." Alex holds out the box, the object inside wrapped ceremoniously in cardboard. Jake takes the box and peeling off the cardboard and the protective sheeting under it.

"I, uh, looked up how to make these," Alex says. "Not sure I got everything right so if it doesn't work, I could prob-ably re-make it—"

"Alex, did you make me a mezuzah?" Jake says the word differently than Alex has been saying it in his mind—me-*zuhz*-a and not me-*zoo*-za, but the look in his eyes is worth it.

"Yeah," Alex says. "I thought, maybe it'd help this feel like home."

Jake places the mezuzah gently back on the tissue paper, then gets up and comes over, gripping Alex by the sweater-covered parts of his forearms. "We can put it up on the door later"—because that much was clear in Alex's research, that each major room in a house needed a mezuzah with a scroll carrying blessings—"but this is already home."

And Alex aches to kiss him, once, long and slow, even as he knows he shouldn't.

"Can I try something?" Jake asks.

Alex nods and gets the shock of Jake's bare fingers underneath his chin, something they don't attempt unless Jake is well and truly drained of ghosts. Nothing happens— just the stroke of Jake's fingers along his jaw.

"Here," Jake says, and tilts Alex's chin up, kissing him. A memory comes with it, Alex sitting up in bed one morning, drinking coffee and reading a book shirtless, and the look on his own face when Jake walked in with a pastry asking if he wants a refill. "I've been working on that—only sending the memories I want. It's not perfect and I don't know if it will always work but—"

Alex kisses him again, deep, fingers threading in his hair.

"I guess we'll just have to keep practicing," Jake finishes. "How long until we're good at it?"

Alex pulls back and smiles as Jake rests his forehead against his, nothing passing between them but affection. "We'll just have to find out."

AFTERWORD

Thank you for reading! I hope you enjoyed spending time with Zach and Eugenio, and Alex and Jake as much as I did. And if you want to know more about my other books, including BREAKOUT YEAR, my upcoming publication in 2025 (a standalone Jew4Jew fake dating romance), be sure to subscribe to my newsletter: www.kdcaseywrites.com. (You also get a free story!)

ALSO BY KD CASEY

Unwritten Rules Series

UNWRITTEN RULES, an emotional second-chance baseball romance debut!

FIRE SEASON, an emotional "they were roommates!" friends-to-lovers romance.

DIAMOND RING, a sexy, friends-to-enemies-to-lovers baseball romance.

Standalone

ONE TRUE OUTCOME, a sexy, veteran/rookie romance!

BREAKOUT YEAR, a friends-reunited fake dating romance coming 2025!

Dirty Players

(Co-authored with Lauren Blakely)

DIRTY SLIDE, a grumpy/sunshine, rivals-to-lovers, sexy standalone novella.

DIRTY STEAL, a one-bed-in-the-room, teammates-to-lovers novella.

ABOUT THE AUTHOR

KD Casey (linktr.ee/KDCaseyWrites) is a romance author and baseball fan living in the Washington, DC area. Come talk baseball and writing on Instagram at @KDCaseyWrites.